"I'm sorry to barge in on you," Cleo said.

She approached the large desk slowly. "I'm—" she began tentatively, but the rest of her sentence was left in midair as the man behind the desk raised his head and she met the very blue eyes of Pierre Morelon.

It couldn't be, she thought frantically while making a valiant effort to stem her racing thoughts.

What form of hoodoo had been placed upon herself and this man so that they were inevitably tied together?

Her mind refused to function. Cara just stood there staring at the man the village chief had "married" her to six years ago. The man who, in a primitive Polynesian ceremony, had become her husband....

OTHER
Harlequin Romances
by JANE CORRIE

Many of these titles are available at your local bookseller
or through the Harlequin Reader Service.

For a free catalogue listing all available Harlequin Romances,
send your name and address to:

HARLEQUIN READER SERVICE,
M.P.O. Box 707, Niagara Falls, N.Y. 14302
Canadian address: Stratford, Ontario, Canada N5A 6W2

or use coupon at back of book.

The Island Bride

by

JANE CORRIE

Harlequin Books

TORONTO • LONDON • NEW YORK • AMSTERDAM
SYDNEY • HAMBURG • PARIS

Original hardcover edition published in 1978
by Mills & Boon Limited

ISBN 0-373-02257-3

Harlequin edition published May 1979

CHAPTER ONE

CARA VERNON glanced round the crowded restaurant, and looked back at the entrance again hoping Cathy would not be too late in arriving, for she had a lot of packing to do between now and tomorrow morning.

Of all her friends, it was Cathy she would miss most she thought. Ermyntrude, too, of course, but you couldn't very well call your stepmother a friend, even though she was.

Cara studied the menu once again; Cathy must have been held up, it wasn't like her to be late. Her eyes scanned the by now familiar fare, but her thoughts were not on food and she wished she had been able to persuade Ermyntrude to take a holiday and accompany her to the small island in French Polynesia that was her destination the following morning. The change, Cara thought, would do her good and would enliven her otherwise dull existence.

She frowned slightly, No, that was not strictly true, for dull as it might appear to Cara, it was all that Ermyntrude wanted. The small village in Devon had provided her with enough friends and interests for her simple tastes, and her three Afghans that she regularly entered for local shows and had had great success with, added all she asked of life.

Ermyntrude ought never, mused Cara, to have

married her father, for although Cara had been very fond of her father, she was not unaware of his shortcomings. He had been a very good doctor, but no knight in shining armour where the gentle sex were concerned. It had often occurred to Cara that he had only married Ermyntrude to provide a mother for his only daughter, and to provide himself with a well-ordered household. However, it soon became apparent that it had been a mistake on both sides. His first wife, Cara's mother, had been a nurse, and the marriage had been an exceptionally happy one—a happiness that had ended after only ten years of marriage after a short but painful illness from which her mother had never recovered.

Two years later Dr Vernon had proposed to Ermyntrude, who had been a childhood sweetheart of his, and had been accepted. As so often happens in such marriages, the reality of what had been a childish wish for both of them proved to be a miserable awakening. Cara's father, who had been used to discussing his work with his wife, found Ermyntrude sympathetic, but entirely unable to contribute to whatever subject had been introduced, for the simple reason that she could never concentrate on the conversation long enough to make a suitable reply.

To be quite fair about it, Cara could also see how infuriating this must have been to her father, who had had no time for what he termed 'dizzy women'.

On this thought Cara smiled. There was no denying that Ermyntrude was 'dizzy', but she was also very sweet, and much too kind to be subjected to censure for what, after all, was her natural make-up.

That Cara's father had been of the same opinion was obvious, as he had taken the only possible way out by accepting an appointment in French Polynesia, thus removing himself as far from the scene as was humanly possible.

Cara had accompanied her father, as the then seven-year-old child had refused to be parted from him. Not that he would have left her with Ermyntrude, he had enough on his conscience without foisting his young daughter on her, even though Ermyntrude would not have hesitated to have accepted the responsibility. It was characteristic of her to blame herself for the failure of the marriage, but there was great relief on both sides when it came to the parting of the ways.

A shout of laughter from the table next to hers brought Cara out of her musings, and she glanced towards the table. It appeared that there was some kind of celebration going on and the merry voices of the foursome floated across her silent one with such clarity that she couldn't help overhearing what was said.

The four men were suitably dressed for an evening on the town, and Cara's eyes lingered on the man seated a little to her right and slightly in front of her so that only his profile was presented to her. His deep well-modulated voice was pleasant to listen to, she mused idly, as she heard him order the meal for the four of them, and surmised he must be the host.

She might not have taken a great deal more notice of the men, had she not heard one of them refer to a Polynesian airport and it brought her attention back to the foursome with a certain amount of curiosity, for it was Cara's destination the following morning.

Now, having one eye on the door to watch for Cathy's arrival and an ear tuned towards the table on her right, Cara listened to the gay bantering going on between the men.

The man she had presumed to be host, and in this it seemed she was correct, was being unmercifully teased by his three companions, and seemed to be taking it all in his stride until the name 'Paula' was introduced into the conversation by a lightly framed, 'I think you ought to warn her, old man,' from one of his friends.

This was immediately seconded by another of the men, who added meaningly, 'Could be a trifle difficult at that. Women are strange creatures, you know. Get all sorts of ideas into their heads. Better to own up, Pierre, and get it over with,' he advised happily.

The man addressed as Pierre did not find this amusing, and showed it by his terse reply. 'I can't think what prompted me to mention the affair in the first place,' he ground out. 'And I don't intend to have the evening ruined by such recollections, if you please.'

'Oh, don't mind Charles,' interjected the fourth member of the party. 'He's only jealous. All that cash, and a beautiful island bride into the bargain —not to mention the delectable Paula grinding her teeth in the background!'

If this remark was calculated to throw oil on troubled waters it sadly misfired, for the said Pierre growled softly but menacingly, 'Leave it, Roger, or I'll leave you to settle the bill!'

The threat finally settled the matter and the talk turned to other topics, not that Cara was listening now, she was too engrossed with her thoughts—thoughts that made her snatch up her bag and drag her coat off the chair opposite her and head for the door of the restaurant, almost colliding with Cathy as she entered.

'Too crowded,' she gasped out at the startled Cathy, and without giving her a chance to prove her wrong, she pulled her through the door and out on to the street.

Cathy's big blue eyes studied Cara's over-bright brown ones and slightly flushed cheeks. 'But we have a table,' she protested. 'I ordered one, didn't I?'

Ignoring this proven fact, Cara cast a look down the street endeavouring to find another restaurant, and spotting a neon sign in the distance, said quickly, 'Let's try the Troubadour, I've heard the food's very good there.'

'Liar!' said the now curious Cathy. 'You'd never even heard of it before. Something's up, isn't it? You came out of that place like a bat out of hell. If I didn't know you better I'd say you'd just held up the cashier!'

She gave an elaborate sigh on seeing that her words had not reached through to the still bemused Cara, who stood beside her lost in a reverie of her own.

The words 'island bride' and the name 'Pierre' were still resounding in her brain. It couldn't possibly be a coincidence. It all fitted—the man's name alone was proof enough of this. Pierre was not a common name—and he was going back to French Polynesia. She swallowed. It was ridiculous—the whole thing was ridiculous! She turned to Cathy who was patiently waiting for some recognition of her presence. 'I've got to talk to you, Cathy. You're right, something did happen in there and I must talk to someone about it,' she said worriedly.

Cathy gave her a wary look and sighed heavily. 'And to think I practically ran all the way here after being held up in a traffic jam,' she said a little plaintively. 'I can't think what's worrying you, unless,' she added with the humour back in her voice, 'the waiter tripped over your handbag. You're always leaving it lying around.'

'No, no, it's nothing like that!' Cara answered impatiently, failing for once to respond to Cathy's sense of humour.

It was Cathy's turn to look worried now. She had known Cara for a long time and whatever it was that had happened, it had to be serious to produce this reaction from her. 'Okay, I'm all ears! Let's go back to my place and skip eating out. I'll rustle something up for us.'

Twenty minutes later, Cara sat in Cathy's small bedsitter and listened to the sounds emanating from the tiny kitchenette as Cathy set about preparing a meal for them. It was no use asking if she could help, there was only space for one person to move in comfort in the area. 'Sorry, Cathy,' she called out. 'You're tired. I wish we'd settled for a Chinese take-away or something. I'm not really hungry, you know, but you're probably starving.'

'Too right!' came the answer from Cathy. 'I'm also agog to hear your news—and it had better be good,' she threatened as she emerged from the kitchenette carrying a tray with knives and forks on it

and put it down on a side table. 'I did a stew over
the weekend and put the rest in the fridge. That's
what we're having, it shouldn't take long to heat
up,' she commented as she sat down beside Cara.
'Now give!' she commanded.

Cara frowned in an effort of concentration; how
to start was the problem. It was all so long ago, yet
for a moment or so in that restaurant it had seemed
only yesterday.

'Do you remember when I first came to Merry's?'
she asked Cathy, Merry's being the nickname for the
boarding school that the girls had attended and that
went under the auspicious name of Lady Merri-
dean.

Cathy nodded, and gave Cara a grin. 'You said
you were English, but we had reservations there
—you looked more like a native of the island you'd
come from.'

Cara smiled at this. 'Well, I'd lived there for almost nine years. Remember I told you that my
father was a doctor? I must have been about seven
when he took up an appointment on Totorua.'

She was silent for a second while she marshalled
her thoughts, then sensing Cathy's impatience she
made a hesitant start. 'I didn't want to leave the
island. I was so happy there, I never thought the
day would come when I would have to.' She gave a
small sigh before going on. 'I must explain this part
to you so you can see how things were, otherwise
none of it would make sense.'

Cara looked back at Cathy who sat watching her
with a gleam of anticipation in her eyes. 'I was sixteen when my father died,' she went on slowly, 'he'd
been out fishing and got caught by a tidal wave,'

she gave a small shrug. 'It was just one of the hazards that threaten an otherwise idealistic occupation. For me, it was the end of my world as I'd known it. Not only had I lost someone I loved very much, but I had to face the prospect of coming back to England alone. Oh, I know I had Ermyntrude, and Uncle Theobald, but although I was fond of both of them, neither could provide me with the kind of life I'd been living.'

She gave a wry smile. 'Of the two of them, I think I would have plumped for Uncle Theobald, he and Dad were very much alike. He's got the same outlook on life as my father had, but his health wasn't as good, and being of a bronchial disposition and a bachelor, he couldn't really take me on, and that left Ermyntrude and the village of Lee, and my memories at that time were not what might be considered happy ones of the small Devon village—particularly when compared to a Polynesian village.'

She met Cathy's enquiring look with a small smile. 'Well, the thing was, I couldn't face it. Not at that time, anyway. We didn't live in the village, but the villa we lived in was just on the fringes of it and much of my time was spent associating with the inhabitants, although I was never allowed to forget that I was a European. I had private tuition from an English tutor—Dad saw to that—otherwise, I was allowed plenty of free rein. I even dressed as the village girls did,' she smiled in memory. 'Dad used to call me his dusky beauty, but I had to toe the line when some of his friends called for dinner, or when we went into town for shopping, when I would have to wear conventional clothes.'

She touched her blue-black hair lightly, and grinned at Cathy. 'As you remarked earlier, I could have passed for a native of the islands. It appears I take after my Spanish grandmother—on my mother's side. I only needed a tan, which I soon acquired, and the resemblance was more or less complete.' She frowned at this point. 'So although on the face of it what I'm going to tell you might sound crazy, it isn't, and it did happen.'

The simmering stew that was sending waves of appetising odours through to the small sitting room failed to detract Cathy's attention from Cara's narration, in spite of her confessed hunger.

'I think the climax came for me when Tu-Tu, the chief of the village, visited me a day or so after my father's death. Tu-Tu and my father had been good friends, and he came to tell me that I wasn't to worry about anything—he would see to things for me. He could have left everything to be handled by the hospital Dad worked for, but I suppose he felt he owed it to Dad to do what he could for me. The hospital had told him that my uncle had been told of his brother's death, and that they were waiting to hear from him. I expect they thought he would fly out to the island and take charge of things.'

She sighed lightly. 'I thought the same, and it was all that kept me going for the next few days. I had some idea that when Uncle Theobald saw the island, he would want to stay. It wasn't such a crazy idea at that; he owned an export business in England, and Totorua does a lot of trade in export with various commodities. Besides that, Dad had often said that it would do his health the world of good if he could settle in a warmer climate.' She took a deep breath. 'But it didn't work out like that. He was having one of his bronchial attacks when he got the news, and there was no possibility of his making any journey, let alone one to the other side of the world. What was worse from my point of view was that he wanted me put on the next plane out, and said that he was making arrangements that end to have me met.

'And that was that. There was a plane out at four that afternoon, and I had three hours in which to pack, and say goodbye to Totorua.' She looked at Cathy. 'But I intended doing no such thing. For me, it was three hours' freedom that gave me time to work out a master plan that would enable me to stay on the island. If I could prove to them that I could look after myself and was determined to stay —well, they would have to let me.' She smiled at this remembrance. 'It all seemed so simple then. Of course, I wasn't thinking at all coherently at the time. I only knew I was very unhappy, and if I could only stay on the island everything would be all right.'

She gave Cathy an apologetic look. 'Sorry, dear, to take so long to come to the point, but as I said earlier, unless you can understand how I felt at that time you won't be able to understand the rest of it. There's not much left to tell now, except that as you've probably gathered, I ran away.'

Cara went on to tell her how she had hidden herself away close to a banana plantation where there was plenty of luxuriant growth to hide her movements, and far enough away from the village to avoid discovery. 'There were mountain streams I could fish from. There was fruit on the trees—I'd learnt a lot from the villagers, remember, even how to erect a shelter out of banana leaves. Even if some-one had come across me there, I wouldn't have looked any different from the rest of the island girls. I even had flowers tucked in my hair.'

She narrowed her eyes in thought for a second, then added, 'I suppose I was trying to indoctrinate myself to the ways of the island, not only living like the villagers, but looking like them, too.' She gave a rueful grin. 'So you can imagine how I felt when my cover was blown by an interfering male.' She shrugged. 'Even now, I can still feel the resentment I felt towards him at the time. I must have been away for about three days when he came across me. He certainly didn't know I was English, and told me in a grand manner that I was trespassing, and on seeing that I was completely alone, started asking me more questions. I might have got away with it if he hadn't spotted my roughly built shelter, but he did, and from then on, tried to elicit exactly what I was doing there—and why I was alone.

'I was furious at having been found. I very nearly shouted at him to go away and leave me alone. However, on second thoughts, I realised that when he knew I was English he would do no such thing but drag me back to the authorities. So I made out I didn't know much English. I had a smattering of French, but he spoke so fast I couldn't grasp what he was saying, which was just as well, for it suited my purpose to say as little as possible.'

She sighed at this point. 'As it turned out, it was a stupid thing to do. If I'd told the truth, the ensuing events wouldn't have happened——' her eyes screwed up at this. 'At least, I don't think they would have happened.'

As if loth to go on, she turned her attention to the smell of simmering stew. 'Oughtn't you to take that off the stove?' she said quickly. 'I can tell you the rest after we've eaten.'

Cathy gave a quick gasp and ran for the kitchenette. 'It's okay,' she called back to Cara. 'I was just in time to prevent it burning.' The last words were said as she rejoined Cara. 'As for finishing after we've eaten, not on your life! I've a feeling we're getting to the interesting part—and I've been so patient, haven't I?—but I shall burst soon if you don't get to the point,' she wailed.

Cara grinned at her. 'Very well,' she said. 'I shall just say that my tactics didn't work, and having got the name of the village out of me, he did exactly what I'd been afraid he'd do—dragged me back there. Well,' she conceded, 'not dragged exactly, but he did make me accompany him back to his car and drove me back to the village.' She frowned. 'I did try to get him to drop me off before we reached the village, by making a few signs that I wanted to be put down outside the village, but no such luck! Even then, I might have been able to make myself scarce had not Tu-Tu been in the village square when we drove in.'

She gave Cathy a quick look, and on noting that she was indeed on the point of exploding, swallowed hastily and gabbled out, 'Whereupon he promptly married us!'

There was a tiny hush after this astounding statement, and then Cathy let out a squeak. 'He *what*?'

she got out, and stared at Cara with eyes wide open as she assimilated the news, then she gasped out, 'Oh, come on, Cara! I'll agree that you were very upset at the time, but to say that you were married to this man is impossible! For goodness' sake! And what was he doing all this time?' she demanded.

'Absolutely nothing,' replied Cara, trying to look solemn but failing, for the look on Cathy's face destroyed any such hope. 'He was just as perplexed as I was when Tu-Tu, after demanding to see his credentials, broke into some kind of a Polynesian chant, during which he took the man's handkerchief out of his top pocket and gave it to me, then took one of my flowers out of my hair and gave it to the extremely puzzled man. He then pointed at me and stared at the man, and said *"Vahine"*.'

Cathy's fixed expression gave no sign of enlightenment, so Cara was forced to explain. '*Vahine*,' she said softly, 'means "wife", in Polynesian.'

'I just don't believe it!' said the sorely tried Cathy. 'I mean, not in this day and age. That kind of thing might have been possible years ago, but not now.'

'That's what the man said,' answered Cara, now back to whatever was worrying her. 'He was fully aware of what the word meant, and proceeded to read the riot act to the chief. For a while there we were even, he was just as furious then as I'd been earlier when he'd insisted on bringing me back to the village. As for the "marriage", I didn't believe in it either. I thought the old chief was trying it on, as it were. When I thought about it later, I realised it was his way of protecting my honour, in case I'd

lost it, I mean. He knew very well that he couldn't
hold the man to the marriage—if I'd been a vil-
lager, it would have been a different matter. He
was a chief, and the old ways are still used on the
odd occasion. In this case, I believe he was trying
to instil some measure of conscience into the man—
just in case anything had happened, since in a sense
he felt responsible for me.

'Looking at it from his point of view,' she went
on musingly, 'it does make sense. I was away for
three days, then I suddenly appeared in this man's
company. He was also well aware of the European
outlook on such matters, and it was his way of trying to put things right.'

Cathy nodded slowly at this, then gave a quick
grin. 'I don't suppose this man appreciated his point
of view at the time, though, do you?'

'Hardly,' replied Cara dryly. 'He was hopping
mad, and threatened to report Tu-Tu to the
authorities. He also said he was due to leave for the
U.K., the following day, but would make certain
the affair was reported before he left. I can only
remember feeling terrified that Tu-Tu would suggest that I accompany him, and the fat would really
have been in the fire then. However, I think
Tu-Tu had the sense to let well alone, although
the news did please him, seeing that I too was going
home shortly. I've wondered since if it would have
made any difference if I'd spoken up and assured
the chief that I was unharmed, and that the man
had only been trying to help me by bringing me
back, but to be honest, I was too miserable, and
not a bit sorry for him. If he'd left me alone he
wouldn't be in this mess, I told myself, and if we

were married it would serve him right for interfering, so I said nothing.'

Cathy sat back and surveyed her friend. 'And to think,' she said, 'that I thought I knew all about you. Now she calmly tells me she's had a shotgun wedding—if that doesn't beat everything!' she grinned. Suddenly a thought struck her and she gave Cara a quick look. 'That restaurant,' she said swiftly. 'Don't tell me—let me guess—you met the man you were married to!'

Cara blinked in surprise at this near-truth, and Cathy gave a delighted crow of triumph. 'You did!' she said, but added appealingly as if she couldn't really believe it, 'Did you—honestly?'

'I didn't,' admitted Cara slowly, 'actually meet him, but I sat at the next table to his.'

Cathy clasped her hands in an expression of anticipation. 'Well, go on!' she demanded. 'Did he recognise you?'

Cara shrugged. 'I doubt if he even saw me. You see, he was sitting a little in front of my table, so I only saw his profile, and unless he was actually looking in my direction, which he wasn't, he couldn't have seen me.'

Cathy was disappointed, but still curious. 'If you saw only his profile, how do you know it was him?' she asked, then brightened slightly as an idea hit her. 'He must be awfully good-looking to have made such an impression on you after all these years. Let me see—it's six years, isn't it?'

The bland amused way Cathy was taking things began to irritate Cara, although she had to admit that if she had been in Cathy's position she too would have seen the funny side of it, but as it was she was unable to share that amusement. 'I have no idea,' she began stiffly, 'whether he's good-looking or not. In fact, if we passed in the street in broad daylight I wouldn't recognise him.'

'Of course you wouldn't, dear,' soothed Cathy hopefully, but spoilt it all by commenting brightly, 'I expect it was something to do with the way he held his head—they say it's odd little mannerisms like that that stick in the mind.'

Cara tried to assume an indignant expression at this double-edged comment, but failed, and gave a strangled chuckle. 'Oh, Cathy! It isn't funny! If you'd been with me and heard what I heard, you'd understand. It was the conversation that drew my attention to the table in the first place. There was I, watching the restaurant door and hoping you wouldn't be too late, and just going through what I had to do before I left tomorrow, when I heard my island mentioned. I wasn't eavesdropping,' she explained, 'I simply couldn't help overhearing what was said, and as it was some kind of celebration it was rather a noisy party.'

She frowned as she recalled what had been said. 'It appeared that one of the four men was going there, and it was a sort of a farewell do. Well, anyway, after I heard that, I was naturally curious, it was a bit of a coincidence, after all, but when they teased the man who was going about his "island bride" and how someone named Paula ought to be warned about her—all in innocent fun, mind you —the man was simply furious, and said something about wishing he'd never mentioned the affair in the first place, and he had no wish to discuss it, etc. . . .' She looked down at the carpet at her feet.

'The man's name was Pierre,' she added dismally.
'And the man that brought me back to the village
was also named Pierre—and that was all I did remember about him—as I told you, I was too miserable at that time to remember much, except how I
might have got away with it if he hadn't turned up.'

Cathy studied Cara's bent head as she concen-
trated her gaze on the carpet. It was odd really, she
thought, if anyone else had told her a story like that,
she would have accused them of slightly under-
rating her intelligence—anyone, that was, but Cara,
whom she knew a little too well to doubt her word.
Remembering too how she had looked when she
had first appeared at the school, it was not hard for
Cathy to visualise her in a sarong, complete with
flowers in her lovely blue-black hair. Her brown
eyes with the unusual amber flecks in them, that
were now so seriously watching her, had denoted
warmer climates than those endured in England.
The Spanish factor of course had given the illusion
added credence. 'I don't see why you're so worried,'
she said calmly. 'It's not as if it was a real marriage,
is it? And for all you know the poor man might
have already had a wife—have you thought of that?
It might be this Paula they were talking about.'

Seeing that her commonsense approach had failed
to take the worried look off her friend's face, she
added with a touch of asperity, 'Come on, Cara! For
goodness' sake! It was six years ago—and no one in
their right mind would attach any importance to it.
As for you haring out of that restaurant like that—
well, really! If you didn't recognise the man, do
you think he would recognise you? Of course not!'
She studied her critically. 'Your hair's the same

colour, of course, but the way you now wear it, twisted up into that huge bun thing, makes you look just what you are—a highly proficient qualified physiotherapist.' She grinned at this, then went on quickly, 'Also, you've lost that tan, and I defy any-one to link you now with a tropical island of any kind.'

Cara gave her a weak grin. 'From one highly proficient qualified physiotherapist to another, I thank you for the compliment. However,' she added, now solemn again, 'I entirely agree with you about the time lapse, also about anyone attaching any importance to the affair—because I certainly didn't, but if you could have heard the way the man took umbrage at the remarks passed, you'd be worried too. As for being already married—well, I doubt it. Not that he was that young or anything like that, but I have a shrewd suspicion that old chief Tu-Tu would have known this before he performed the ceremony. I know he had a few questions he wanted answering by the man, and it was a conversation carried out in French that I didn't attempt to unravel. I only know it made the man even more furious than he was before. Don't you see?' she queried of Cathy. 'Supposing he's not married, but is engaged to this girl—and just supposing he's not absolutely sure whether the ceremony old Tu-Tu performed was in fact legal?'

'Oh, Cara!' broke in Cathy indignantly. 'He can't be that dumb!' she insisted. 'He said he was going to report him to the authorities, didn't he? Well, he would have been reassured on this point, for a start.'

'But supposing he didn't have time to see anyone?' persisted Cara. 'He was going back to the U.K. the next day, wasn't he? It wouldn't leave him much time to arrange an appointment. Besides,' she mused thoughtfully, 'it would have been a bit embarrassing for him, wouldn't it? I was missing for three days, remember, and I hadn't attempted to explain to Tu-Tu that he'd only found me that morning, so he couldn't have had much hope of my backing up his statement where the Governor was concerned.'

'Well, that's it, then!' said Cathy with a gleam of enlightenment in her eyes. 'Embarrassment, of course! It's hardly the sort of thing one would want brought out when one was engaged, would it? Still, I don't think he's going the right way about it at all if he's trying to hush it up. It will only make more out of it than there really was. Women love mysteries, and this Paula is no exception, I'll bet. One whiff of intrigue and she'll be on the trail like a foxhound. He doesn't,' she told Cara dryly, 'seem to be very well informed on the feminine character. What a pity you couldn't have gone over to their table and introduced yourself,' she added with a grin. 'Particularly as you seem to be so sure that that Pierre was the same Pierre the old chief married you to. Mind you, it would have caused a bit of a sensation if it wasn't the same man,' she chuckled.

Cara gave her an exasperated look. 'If I hadn't been sure, I would have stayed in the restaurant,' she told her crossly, 'and not hared out like that. I'm not that much of a harebrain, am I?' she demanded. 'As for introducing myself,' she visibly shuddered, 'if it had been you, I suppose that's just what you would have done, but not me. I was so shaken and so appalled that anyone could have taken such an attitude towards what could be termed as a farcical interlude that I just took off. What's really worrying me is that he might be going back to the island to make some enquiries. For all I know he might be worried about this Paula finding out, especially if he intends to settle there. It was a farewell do, remember, and,' she added grimly, 'can you imagine what effect such enquiries would have on my job? The island isn't all that large—and he knows where the village is.' She gave Cathy a gloomy look. 'It would be a good start for me, wouldn't it? No matter how you look at it, it's bound to start some kind of speculation should the wretched business ever come to light.'

'Well,' commented Cathy ruminatingly, 'from what you've told me, this Pierre is as anxious as you are to forget the whole business. Honestly, Cara, I shouldn't worry about it. Chances are he won't bother to make any enquiries—not unless he's looking for trouble.' She brightened as a thought struck her. 'Perhaps he's just got a job out there, too, and if so, he'll be as anxious as you are to bury the past. I think you're making mountains out of molehills, dear,' she said gently. 'I admit you've had a shock, but for goodness' sake keep things in perspective. You'll probably never see him again and in a few months' time you'll be wondering why you got so worked up.'

CHAPTER TWO

THE following morning when Cara sat in the airport lounge waiting for her flight, she listened a little absentmindedly to Ermyntrude's vague meanderings on how she must write to her as soon as possible, and to be sure to give her regards to her Uncle Theobald for her, and how she wished she were not going so far away.

Cara said, 'yes', or 'no', in the appropriate places, smiling a little to herself at Ermyntrude fussing over her, but her thoughts were elsewhere, centred on the island she was returning to after so long away. There was a sense of excited anticipation, much as one would have when returning home.

Her earlier fears of a meeting with the man named Pierre had vanished with the morning light. She had Cathy to thank for this, her good sense and sound reasoning had dispelled her worries. She was right, of course, Cara mused, and she couldn't think why she had let herself get into such a panic for nothing. It must have been the shock of hearing about it after so long that had slightly unbalanced her reasoning; she was not usually so stupid.

As she watched some late arrivals rush through the lounge towards the checking-in counter, she thought how lucky she had been in getting the job she had applied for at her father's old hospital. The fact that her father had worked for the hospital had given her application added leverage, she knew, and she was grateful for it. Cathy too had the job she wanted, working for a rather exclusive health farm somewhere in the wilds of Norfolk, and not too far from her home town, and she had promised Cara to take a trip out to see her one summer during her holiday period.

With a small sigh of happy anticipation, she glanced up at the departure board. Her flight should soon be announced. She turned her full attention back to Ermyntrude who had not been talking for a few seconds, and found her studying a man and a woman who had just entered the lounge.

'I say,' said Ermyntrude in a stage whisper, 'isn't that Paula Ericson, the concert pianist?'

Not having the slightest idea of whether Ermyntrude was right or not, Cara could hardly confirm the question, but looked at the woman anyway. She was tall, dark, and very lovely, and was dressed in a cool shantung silk suit of burnt orange colouring. Ermyntrude could be right at that, Cara thought, for there was a certain air about the woman that spoke of an aplomb that comes from constant stage appearances. It wasn't that she asked for attention, her looks alone would have guaranteed this. It was that indefinable something that separated the successful from the unsuccessful, no matter what profession they followed.

'I'm certain it is!' said Ermyntrude, now sounding excited. 'Oh, I wish I'd got the courage to go up and thank her for the immense pleasure her music has given me,' she sighed.

Cara was about to suggest that she was sure she

wouldn't mind such congratulations, for if she were Paula Ericson then she must be used to such attention, when her eyes were drawn to the man beside the concert pianist, who at that moment had turned to look at the departure board, and Cara was able to see his face quite clearly. One look was enough to dispel the encouragement she had been about to give Ermyntrude, for the man was the last man Cara wanted to meet, accidentally or otherwise!

Cara's whole attention was now directed on the man as he spoke to his companion. As Ermyntrude was certain that the woman was Paula Ericson, so Cara was certain of the identity of the man beside her. The autocratic manner he had of raising his eyebrows was one thing she did remember about him.

'Still,' went on Ermyntrude, 'it would be rather an imposition, wouldn't it? It's not as if she'd just given a performance, is it? She has some privacy; it's just that I have such an admiration for her work.' She gave a little gasp as a thought struck her. 'Do you think she might be travelling on the same plane as you?' she asked Cara.

'I don't know about her,' replied Cara before she could stop herself, 'but I know he is!'

Ermyntrude stared at her. 'Do you know him?' she asked hopefully.

It was too late to regret her words now, and all Cara could do was to think up some plausible cover for this lapse on her part. 'Well, I don't really,' she hedged, 'but I'm only going by the case he's carrying. I mean, a briefcase wouldn't be the sort of luggage she would travel with, would it? And she hasn't as much as a vanity case with her, has she?'

she added vaguely in an effort to add weight to her theory.

'How clever of you to notice that,' replied Ermyntrude admiringly, making Cara cast a quick glance at her and wonder if she were being facetious, but she ought to have known that Ermyntrude was sincere. It was only her guilty conscience that prompted the suspicion! 'Now I'd never notice things like that,' continued Ermyntrude confidingly, then sighed reminiscently, 'but then you're like your father, he was clever, too.'

To Cara's relief, the flight she was waiting for was flashed on the board, and she gave Ermyntrude a farewell hug before she followed the rest of the passengers out of the main airport lounge and through to the departure lounge.

Before she disappeared from view, Cara turned to give Ermyntrude one last wave, and collided with the man behind her who had the same intention in mind. Her cheeks flushed pink when she turned to apologise and found herself staring at the man Pierre, not that he was looking at her, for his whole attention was focused on the woman who stood a little in front of Ermyntrude, and who blew him a kiss from her delicately tinted lips.

As Cara was about to turn down the corridor, she heard the woman call out in a pleasant husky voice, 'Don't rescue any more damsels in distress, will you, darling?'

The words made Cara freeze on the spot, and she cast a hasty glance back at the man who was staring back at the woman with an expression on his face that spoke of annoyance, and Cara received the definite impression that he would have liked to query this remark, but had no other option but to proceed on his way as there were several people behind him.

As her eyes followed his tall figure as he boarded the plane ahead of her, Cara underwent a variety of emotions. So much for Cathy's assertion that the affair was forgotten! The only thing she had been right about was that the man had not recognised her, in spite of the fact that she had cannoned into him. Cara even doubted if he had looked at her, he was too intent on the lovely brunette who was waving him farewell.

Her thoughts careered on as she absentmindedly took the seat the stewardess indicated she should occupy, and it would not have surprised her to find herself sitting right next to the cause of her present discomfort. The way things were going, Cara had a nasty suspicion that had their destination been Australia or some other vast continent, she would still have found herself running into the man!

Ordinarily, she was not superstitious, but she couldn't help pondering on the extraordinary turn of events that had catapulted her back into this man's life again.

A day or so ago she had completely forgotten his existence, as she had the episode that had thrown them together, and had she met him later on the island, she would not have known him as the man Tu-Tu had 'married' her to, for the simple reason that she had attached no importance to the event, and if reminded, would have shrugged the incident off as farcical, as indeed she was sure the man concerned would have done too. If he had been allowed to, of course, she reminded herself, remembering his curt dismissal of the subject.

In her mind's eye Cara saw his face again, and that characteristic way he had of raising his brows, not so much in query as in hauteur. A proud man, she thought.

Her frown deepened as she considered his position; all in all, she rather felt sorry for him, for it was obvious that some well-meaning friend had dropped the delectable Paula a subtle hint as to what had happened, and she was now as Cathy had so aptly put it, 'on the trail like a foxhound'.

'Are you all right, dear?' queried the woman sitting next to Cara, staring at her anxiously, adding kindly, 'I've a magazine here if you'd like to read it, in case you're worried about the flight, that is.'

Cara's frown quickly dispersed as she gave the woman a smile of reassurance. 'No, thanks,' she said quickly. 'As I've been lucky enough to get a seat by the window, I want to look out. It's just,' she explained to the woman, 'that I'm wondering whether I cancelled all the things I ought to have cancelled —you know how it is in the last-minute rush,' she confided with a grin.

'Don't I just!' answered the woman with a grimace. 'No matter how much notice one has, one always forgets something!'

The rest of the flight passed pleasantly enough for Cara, and although she kept a wary eye open for the man named Pierre, she did not see him again, not even after they landed at the small airport, but by that time she was too excited at the thought that she would soon be home to worry about other matters. However, one thing she did promise herself, and that was that should she ever have the opportunity of meeting the man who had taken her back to the village, or as his Paula had intimated, 'rescued her', then she would make a point of introducing herself, and treat the whole thing as a joke, thus removing any doubt or worry on his part of any liability incurred.

A tired but very happy Cara stepped down the gangway after the plane had landed, and her eyes lit up as she saw the large form of her uncle hovering near the arrival bay, and rather startled him by her exuberant welcome as she flung her arms around his portly figure and gave him a hug.

'Oh, Uncle Theo! It's so nice to be home again,' she exclaimed with eyes sparkling with the hint of tears. 'I've been so worried that something would crop up to stop me coming,' she gave a chuckle. 'Or that I would fail my finals!' Her hand squeezed his arm. 'But I didn't—and here I am!' she said happily.

Her uncle's blue eyes that so reminded her of her father twinkled back at her as he remarked dryly, 'I'm fully aware that you have arrived, although,' he added on a serious note, 'if you hadn't got yourself a job lined up, I might have advised you to stay where you were.'

Cara's surprised eyes met his swiftly, and she said worriedly, 'Have you been ill again?' thinking as she said this that he looked in the best of health. Her father had spoken the truth when he had said that the climate would suit his brother's health, and he must have passed on this suggestion to him, since Theo had decided to accept his advice, and had taken up residence there a few years later.

At the time, the news had not come as a welcome

surprise to Cara, who was still of the opinion that had he arrived a little earlier, she might well still be living on Totorua. This rather biased point of view was soon replaced by a more practical one. She could not have spent her life idling on the golden beaches, living as a nomad, as she had so fondly imagined herself doing all those years ago. There were of course facilities for her to take the same examinations, and follow the career she had set her sights on, but in her heart of hearts she knew she would not have conformed to the necessary training long enough to achieve her ambition—there would have been too many distractions. As it was, she had been so miserable that she had thrown herself into her studies. Failure was not to be contemplated—not when so much depended upon it, namely, her return to the island.

Her worried glance remained fixed on her uncle as she waited for his reply to her query, and her frown relaxed a little as she saw him give her a lopsided grin.

'Oh, I'm well enough, no cause for concern in that direction, I'm thankful to say,' he said as he relieved her of her overnight case, and gently steered her towards the baggage collection area. 'We'll talk about it later,' he said.

The following morning, Cara relaxed in the cane chair on the patio that adjoined the dining room of the villa, and savoured the sweet-scented air that drifted towards her from the numerous flowers now at their height of beauty, for it was the island's summer.

Her wondering gaze rested on the bright panorama before her, and even though she had witnessed other summer displays in the past, the sheer beauty of the blossoms never failed to reach a chord in her heart. The winter there bore no comparison to the winters she had known in England. It was more of a rest for certain shrubs, while others carried on the display. She took a deep breath and recalled the numerous occasions she had tried to describe a scene such as the one she was now viewing to Cathy, but had not been able to convey a fraction of the wondrous sight. It was not possible, she mused, or justifiable to even try. One had to witness such sights to believe in them. Each season had its own display, its own special beauty. The ancient waterfalls in the tropical forests ensured enough moisture for the exotic plants to thrive, and it was no wonder that the early explorers of the islands were of the opinion that they had found paradise.

A slight breeze rustled the leaves of a breadfruit tree, and Cara's gaze rested there for a moment or two. The olive green of the large leaves shone in the rays of the sun as if polished by a diligent worker. The lighter green of the fruit, with its rough almost prickly-looking covering, hung below the leaves as if inviting one to pick them. Her gaze travelled on to a flowering tree that was really a shrub but had grown to such large proportions through the favourable climate that it was now a tree. Its bright pink blossoms almost eclipsed its foliage, parts of which could be seen peeping out under the large glossy flower blooms.

A little way beyond the flame tree, or to use its correct botanical name, the Royal poinciana, was another flowering shrub, again of tree proportion, that seemed to be competing for attention with its scarlet pointed blossoms, not quite so large as the poinciana, but of such brilliant hue that the eye was drawn towards it. This was a red ixora, sometimes called Jungle Flame by the islanders.

Cara let out a sigh of pure contentment; as beautiful as they were, they were only part of nature's constant exhibition to delight the eye and formed a backcloth for other just as wonderful colourful plants. She tore her gaze away from the tree blossoms and looked at a group of yellow flowers nestling in a corner of the garden. These were named Birds of Paradise, and so called because their delicate petals grew upwards and branched out, and did indeed resemble a bird in flight. A short distance away, in direct contrast to the brilliant yellow, was a cluster of scarlet blossoms, that hung down in long clusters resembling bright tassels, and this was the chenille plant—or Pussy Tail, to use its more familiar name.

There were the dwarf poincianas of an orange hue, various shades of orchid, ranging from a delicate pink to a satiny mauve. To add a note of sobriety in the otherwise riotous background was a clump of white agaparithis that mingled with other wondrous plants too numerous to name.

Her breath was expelled slowly at the thought that she was home at last, and this time she would stay. Not even the unwelcome news her uncle had had to impart to her the previous evening could dispel her quiet happiness in her homecoming.

A tiny sigh escaped her as her wide brown eyes with the tawny gold specks in them centred on the white strip of the airport runway that she could see even from where she sat on the patio, and moved on to the impressive white buildings in the distance that formed the airport.

She had never envisaged such a happening coming to pass, but then she had been unaware that the villa had not been bought by her father, but only leased to him by a grateful patient. She stared at the cool area around her, at the greeny-blue marble flecked tiles at her feet, and on to the ornamental verandah from which hung festoons of a deep purple bougainvillaea that emanated a heady scent that permeated the patio. She had taken so much for granted, and could hardly blame her uncle for spoiling what otherwise would have been a happy homecoming.

It was not his fault that she had been ignorant of the fact that they did not own the villa. If it had not been for the man who had wished to show his gratitude to her father for saving his life, they would have had to live in one of the numerous hostels provided for such contingencies—she swallowed painfully—and where she herself would now have to live.

Even if her father's patron had still been living, it was doubtful whether Cara would have been granted permission to stay at the villa. As it was, his son, who had inherited the vast business empire from his father, the airport being just one of the numerous enterprises now under construction, had plans to convert the villa into an hotel to accommodate the airport passengers who required overnight stays.

All this Cara had learnt from her uncle the previous evening; he appeared to take a philosophical view towards the new owner's decision to turn the villa into an hotel. 'We were lucky to have had it for as long as we had,' he had told the partially stunned Cara, who wondered how he could have been so matter-of-fact about it. Afterwards, it had occurred to her that he had acquired the islanders' happy-go-lucky disposition that eventually affected all inhabitants, and only wished she could adopt a carefree attitude towards the news. Given a little more time perhaps she would, but the villa was more than a home to her, it was a place of nostalgia and precious memories of her father.

When her uncle also told her of his arrangements to settle down in one of the island's select clubs that catered for bachelors, she was able to understand his attitude over the loss of the villa. The courtesy extended to her father from his patron had also encompassed his brother, and a position in an exporting firm had been offered him and gratefully accepted, thus making it possible for him to reside on the island, but as he had pointed out to Cara, jobs were not all that easy to obtain, priority being given firstly to the local people, and then to the citizens of the mother country, France.

Considering all this, Cara had to grudgingly concede that she had been fortunate indeed in obtaining a post there, but it hardly helped to lessen her disappointment over losing the villa.

When the cheerful Polynesian woman who was employed by her uncle to cook and clean for him came to clear the breakfast table, Cara took the opportunity of enquiring after the villagers, and learnt that the villa was not the only casualty to fall to the airport requirements. Where the village had once stood, now stood the outbuildings of the airport, the villagers being moved to another village several miles away.

Raua, as she shyly told Cara her name, came from a small settlement a mile or so away from the villa, and was unable to answer Cara's queries, and after she had left to resume her duties in the kitchen, Cara gave a sigh of regret. Six years was not really a long time, but so much had happened between the time she had left and her return that it might as well have been twenty years. There was a saying, she thought sadly, that went something like, 'Never for ever', and in this case it was certainly true.

Monsieur Morelon, the son of her father's patron, had not allowed sentiment to stand in his way, but then, she thought sadly, from what she had heard about him from her uncle, he had spent most of his time away from Totorua, receiving not only an education but a solid background in the commercial line managing his father's varied interests abroad, so it was hardly likely that he had developed any feelings for the island apart from a commercial outlook. The airport was very probably needed, for tourism was a stable source of income to Totorua, and although it had an airport already in existence, extensions were needed to cope with the tourist boom, but like everyone else who agreed with the principle, Cara wished another site had been chosen other than the one on her doorstep.

A swift glance at her watch shook her out of her musings, for she had an appointment at the hospital in just under an hour and was still in her dressing gown, and if she didn't hurry she would not be

ready for the taxi her uncle had ordered for her to
take her into town.

After a quick shower she made a swift inventory
of her wardrobe, and decided to wear her primrose-
coloured two-piece. It was very plain, yet smart, and
she was anxious to make a good impression at her
first appearance before her future employers.

Precisely an hour later she was glad she had taken
pains to present a businesslike appearance to the
Matron of the hospital who was interviewing her.

She welcomed Cara in what might be termed as
a distinctly cool manner, giving the impression that
even though her application had been accepted by
the board of directors, it was by no means certain
that she had obtained the post. This attitude slightly
puzzled Cara, for she had the letter of acceptance
tucked away in her handbag which she was now
gripping hard in an effort to keep her temper.

'I note,' said the Matron in what was almost a
tone of disapproval, 'that your father worked for the
hospital. That,' she told Cara, 'was before my time.'

Here again Cara received the impression that it
was on these grounds alone that she had obtained the
post, in spite of her excellent qualifications. It
also told her that the Matron was of the opinion that
the board of directors had gone over her head in
making the appointment. This was borne out by her
slightly aggrieved remark of, 'I really did not see the
necessity of a full-time appointment in this capac-
ity. We have had a part-time assistant with nurses
who are capable of handling such work, though not
as yet qualified,' she added regretfully.

While Cara watched her as she sorted through
her qualifications she tried to pinpoint the source of

her grievance—for she had a grievance, this much was plain. From her accent, Cara was certain she was French, and while she knew priority for work was given to either the local inhabitants or French citizens, she did not feel it was the sole cause of her offputting manner.

Cara's gaze wandered over the woman who sat in front of her and rested briefly on her smooth features that could have been called lovely if it were not for the petulant pout of the full lips, or the haughty manner, then went over her starched cap perched high on top of her blonde hair. Yes, she was lovely, and the uniform enhanced her femininity, thought Cara. Had she been crossed in love, and would this have produced her sour outlook on life? Well, if she had, Cara was only too relieved that it was nothing to do with her father, for even though he might have been a little on the old side for the woman in front of her, whose age she judged to be around the late twenties, she did know there was some women who preferred older men, and her father had certainly had not only good looks, but a charming manner as well.

She almost jumped when the woman spoke again. 'I also note that apart from the references from your college, you have no local connections. It is usual,' she went on in that same dry tone, that was beginning to get beneath Cara's skin, 'to bring an endorsement from someone in authority here. Not,' she said casually, 'that it's essential, of course,' she shrugged. 'In your case, it might be waived, but it is normal practice here to have such endorsements.'

Cara took due note of the 'might' as the Matron had intended she should. She really was going out of her way to present difficulties for her, she thought furiously, and was tempted to produce the letter that categorically stated that she had obtained the job she had applied for and wave it under this thoroughly unhelpful person's nose. However, there was a certain amount of truth in what she had said, for Cara's father had obtained his appointment through the auspicious help of the late Jean-Paul Morelon, and her uncle had warned her of the difficulty of obtaining work on Totorua.

For this reason only Cara decided to mention Monsieur Morelon, if only to show the woman that her father at least had had impeccable references— not that it would serve to help her to satisfy the Matron's slightly unreasonable attitude towards her appointment, but it would show her that they were not without influential patronage. 'My father's patron was Monsieur Morelon,' she said quietly, feeling a spurt of justified pleasure at the way the name affected the Matron, who changed from a difficult interviewer to an almost gushing friend.

'Monsieur Morelon!' she exclaimed, her cold blue eyes now echoing a much warmer shade. 'Why, I—that is to say, my mother knew him very well— er, Monsieur Jean-Paul Morelon, that is.' She gave a small sigh, and Cara couldn't determine whether it was a sigh of regret at his passing, or a sigh of admiration for his past accomplishments. 'His son is very much like him, don't you think? He was here a few days ago. We're adding another wing to the maternity ward, you know,' she confided to Cara, 'and naturally he is supervising the work. His father not only built the hospital, but supplied many costly additions out of his own pocket.'

As Cara had not personally known either Jean-Paul Morelon or his son, she was forced to remain silent and let the Matron do the talking.

A few minutes later, however, she wished she had explained this to the now friendly Matron, for her bright assumption that Cara need only approach Monsieur Morelon's son to gain the necessary endorsement left Cara in a dilemma.

Had the Matron's attitude been a little less frigid at the start of their acquaintance, Cara might have pointed out that as the man did not know her, it was hardly likely that he would be prepared to vouch for her, even though his father had been her father's patron. As it was, she held her tongue, for something told her that should she be unwise enough to unburden herself at this stage of their acquaintance, she would certainly not receive a sympathetic hearing—the reverse, in fact—and although Cara might have obtained the job—on paper anyway—she was fully aware of the fact that this woman could make life extremely difficult for her in more ways than one; her very position would assure that.

With an inward sigh Cara listened politely as the Matron welcomed her, albeit a little late, to the staff at the hospital, and hoped she would be able to begin her duties the following Monday.

Cara thanked her for her welcome and replied that she was looking forward to the start of her work, and as it was obvious that the interview was now over, she stood up and started to walk to the door. No further mention of the endorsement, or reference, as Cara viewed it, had been made, and she assumed that given enough time the matter would be dropped, and the thought considerably cheered her. The interview had not been an altogether smooth one, but at least Cara had achieved her object and would soon begin her career.

Her happy musings were abruptly curtailed by a remark from Matron as Cara was on the point of leaving the office. 'Do give my regards to Monsieur Morelon, won't you?' she said in what Cara could only describe as a girlish voice, and Cara could only nod in agreement to this innocent-sounding request.

So much for her thinking she could stall her way out of her dilemma, Cara thought wretchedly, and fervently wished she had held her tongue and not mentioned her father's patron. She would still have got the job, she argued silently with herself as she left the hospital and made her way down to the shopping precinct of the town.

The warm sunshine caressed her face as she made her way to a café that had adopted the French style of catering for the customers, with tables spilling out of the café on to the pavement, and protected by the large gay parasols that were almost the hallmark of the mother country.

While Cara slowly sipped the coffee she had ordered, her gaze wandered over the scene before her eyes, though her mind was occupied on other matters, such as finding a way out of the unenviable position she had landed herself in.

The tourists, she noticed, were in full flood, and the gift shops were doing a roaring trade. Street vendors were also making a bid to catch what trade was available, keeping a wary eye out for the roving gendarme, for such trade was frowned upon by the authorities who tried to make certain that the tourists remained unmolested on their tour of the town. The atmosphere was one of happy expectancy, echoed by the gay coloured dresses of the local inhabitants who passed by on their way to the shops. A few women still wore the native *pareu*, although most had adopted the Western style of dress, which was a pity, Cara mused, for the climate alone called for the bright and exceedingly comfortable *pareu* that went under many different names, one being the sarong, as featured in the film world of yesteryear.

With an impatient sigh she jerked herself back to her problem. Somehow she had to have that letter of recommendation, although how she had no idea. Could her uncle help her? she wondered, then gave a slight shake of her head, that was interpreted by the Chinese waiter who was about to fill up her coffee cup as a refusal of more coffee and he went on his way, unnoticed by the reflecting Cara. Her uncle could only suggest that she see Monsieur Morelon who might or might not oblige her, and probably the latter, she thought miserably, fully aware of the imposition she was putting on him.

A look at her watch told her that it was almost twelve o'clock, and hoping her quarry was not participating in an early lunch, she decided to settle the vexed question once and for all. He could only say yes or no, she told herself stoutly as she left the café and proceeded down the shopping precinct in search of his offices, that according to something her uncle had said were to be found somewhere in the vicinity of the quay, and ought not, thought a suddenly quaking Cara, to be too difficult to locate.

CHAPTER THREE

FOR once, Cara was not to stop and admire the breathtaking view from the harbour out to the lagoon beyond the bay, with its blue-green water, so blue in places that it rivalled the clear blue of the sky, and under which lay the beautiful coral in pale iridescent colours protected by the barrier reef beyond that guarded the entrance to the island, and where numerous wrecks lay, their resting place clearly defined by rusting cannon barrels that could still be seen protruding out of the edge of the waterfront where the sea had laid them to rest.

As Cara had thought, it was not difficult to find the offices she sought, and she vaguely wondered how she had not noticed them before, for the premises occupied practically the whole of one side of the busy harbour's commercial section.

All she had to do, she told herself firmly as she entered the main office section of Morelon Enterprises, was ask to see the boss, and if successful, ask him to provide a reference for her on the grounds that his father knew her father. She faltered on this last thought and had to steel herself from about-turning and marching right out again. She wanted that job, didn't she? Not only wanted it, but had to get it to stay on her beloved Totorua. So what was she afraid of? He could refuse, of course, but it wasn't the end of the world, and she would have tried.

With a firm step she walked towards a glass-fronted alcove that was the reception office, and when the aperture slid back to reveal a smiling girl in her early twenties who enquired her business, Cara took the bull by the horns and asked to see Monsieur Morelon.

Asking if she had an appointment and receiving an apologetic no, the girl looked doubtful but was willing to be helpful and said cheerfully, 'You'd better see his secretary,' and directed Cara to an office along the passageway behind the reception area.

So far, so good, thought Cara as she gave the door a firm tap and waited to be admitted. She was over the first hurdle, and was now approaching the second. Having got so far, she did not intend being put off now. Only if Monsieur Morelon was in conference, that was, and there was a valid reason why she should not be granted an interview. It was not as if, she told herself reasonably, she would keep him more than a few minutes. If he agreed to furnish her with a recommendation, it need not necessarily be done there and then, she could call back for it some other time. If the answer was a definite no, then the visit would be of an even shorter duration!

The secretary, a much older woman than the receptionist, had, Cara suspected, been Jean-Paul's secretary as well, for she had the look of long duration about her, as did the office furniture around her, and obviously took her duties seriously as a good secretary should, giving Cara the nasty suspicion that this was one battlement she would be unable to storm. Nevertheless she repeated her request quite firmly even though she was quaking inside.

At the inevitable question, 'What is the nature of your business?' asked in a slightly American accent by the mousy-haired yet glint-eyed secretary, Cara took a deep breath and said, 'Personal.'

At the lift of the eyebrows this statement produced, Cara deduced that the woman did not approve of personal matters entering into office business, and when she sought no further explanation but said dryly that she would see if Monsieur Morelon would see her, Cara was left blinking in surprise at her easy victory over what appeared to be an immovable barricade.

She had still not quite recovered when the secretary reappeared and told her that Monsieur Morelon would see her, but would she be good enough to keep the appointment short as he had an important business lunch date to keep in a quarter of an hour's time.

A slightly breathless but very grateful Cara assured her that she would only keep him a few minutes, and was shown into the adjoining office.

As she approached the large desk in front of her, behind which sat a man whose head was bent over some documents he was studying, her mind was busy working out the right approach to her audacious request, but first she must apologise for her unheralded appearance. 'I do apologise,' she began hastily as the man looked up at her, but the rest of the sentence was left in mid-air as her incredulous eyes met the very blue eyes of Pierre Morelon, the man Tu-Tu had 'married' her to six years ago.

Although she made a valiant attempt to stem her racing thoughts, the uppermost one being that some form of hoodoo had been placed upon herself and this man that inevitably tied them together, she had to go on with the sentence and move a little nearer to the desk, even though she would have preferred to have stayed right where she was near the door. 'I'm sorry to have barged in on you like this,' she said swiftly, realising it was about time she said something, and wondering whether she had her mouth open since that might have accounted for the amused look in his eyes as he waited for her to go on, but her mind simply refused to function and she just stood there feeling foolish.

'Did you come to talk about the villa?' he prompted her gently, obviously taking her silence as embarrassment. 'I presume you are Dr Vernon's daughter?' he added with a smile, holding out a large strong hand towards her, which Cara had to take as she gave a small nod in confirmation. 'Your uncle mentioned that you were returning to To-torua to take up work in the same hospital as your father worked.' He indicated the chair in front of his desk, inviting her to be seated, and Cara was only too grateful to comply as her legs were not as steady as they might have been.

'I'm afraid there is no possibility of our plans being altered at this stage, and while I have every sympathy for your understandable attachment to the villa, its location is ideal for our purpose. I might,' he added musingly, 'be able to find you alternative accommodation—er—nearer the hospital. It is not quite so large, but just as secluded as the villa, and it does have a small garden of sorts, that will ensure you a certain amount of privacy that you would not get in one of the hostels. I under-

stand your uncle has provided himself with accommodation?'

Again Cara gave a small nod, but was only
vaguely aware of the conversation. While she had
listened, her eyes had travelled slowly over the
man's features, marvelling how much she had remembered about him, even though she had told
Cathy that she remembered nothing, and would
have passed him in the street without recognising
him. The habit he had of raising his eyebrows, for
one thing, when he was making a point, and the
very blueness of his eyes that seemed to look right
through you—she caught herself up sharply; she
must have her mouth open again, as he had stopped
talking and was now sitting patiently awaiting her
reply.

'I ... it's very good of you,' she got out swiftly,
almost babbling the words in her anxiety not to
give her thoughts away. 'I haven't got the job yet—
at least,' she added breathlessly, 'I have on paper,
and I thought everything was settled, but the
Matron seemed to require a reference of sorts,' carrying on hastily as she saw his expressive brows raise
slightly, 'Oh, I have references, of course, but she
wants one from a local source. A sort of patron, I
suppose—so I wondered . . .?' she ended lamely, not
knowing how else to put it.

To her almost hysterical relief he nodded com-
placently. 'And you would like me to furnish you
with one?' he asked.

'I know it's a cheek,' she answered apologetically.
'I mean, you hardly know me—well,' she amended
quickly, 'my character anyway, but I couldn't think
of anyone else.'

Pierre Morelon smiled at her and Cara's heart did a somersault. He was handsome—no wonder the Matron had thawed at the mention of his name! 'Very well, Cara. I shall take you on trust.' His eyes lost some of their amusement as they swept round the office. 'It would have been what my father would have wanted,' he said on a gentle note, and pressed a button on his desk.

Within minutes a bemused Cara sat listening to the directions Pierre Morelon was giving his secretary. 'Type out a reference for this young lady, would you, Miss Durand? Say that I have known her family for several years and have no hesitation in recommending her for the post of . . .' he glanced back at Cara, who was still finding it hard to believe that all this was actually happening, and jerked out of her reverie long enough to answer, 'Physiotherapist,' in a dazed way.

She was still in a partial daze when she left his office a short while later, after profusely thanking him for his help, thanks that were waved away by the mildly amused Pierre.

After giving the secretary a few more relevant details, Cara waited while the reference was typed out, and left the offices shortly afterwards wanting to pinch herself to ascertain that she wasn't dreaming. She hadn't really expected to be so successful— or to meet with such courtesy. Pierre Morelon must have thought a lot of his father, she mused, as she walked back to the town, and recalled the look of sorrow in his eyes as he had spoken of him. It was plain that he missed him as much as Cara had missed her father.

Having no further business in the town, she took

a taxi back to the villa, and after a light lunch settled herself in the shade of the patio.

With the events of the morning behind her, she was able to assemble her thoughts in peace, a peace borne out by the secure knowledge that all was well. She had no worries now that her job might be in jeopardy, and could turn up for duty the following Monday armed with the necessary reference—and not only that, she told herself drowsily as the warmth of the sun pervaded the patio; she had no worries over finding herself other accommodation —even that had been taken care of by the kindly Pierre Morelon. A slight frown creased her smooth forehead at the thought that she had not really answered his query as to whether she wanted to accept the alternative accommodation he had in mind for her.

Then the frown was replaced by a slow smile of utter content. He would arrange it for her anyway, she was sure of it. Her sleepy glance took in the patches of sunlight that played on the tiled surface of the patio floor. Yes, she would miss the villa, she thought with a gentle sigh, but one couldn't have everything, and she had been so lucky she had no cause for complaint.

Her thoughts then turned to Cathy, and she wondered how she was faring in her new job. Another small smile lit her features as she envisaged her amazement when told of the extraordinary turn of events, and that Cara had had to apply to her 'husband' for a reference!

Her head rested against the cushion of the chair back. She ought to write to Cathy, but not today, she told herself sleepily; perhaps tomorrow. She had a whole week of leisure before she started work, so there was plenty of time to catch up on her correspondence. Kind Ermyntrude would be looking for a letter, too, and Cara wondered how she had got on at the local show and hoped she had been successful in getting either a first or a second placing for her dogs.

Inevitably her thoughts returned to her interview with Pierre Morelon that morning. What an extremely charming man he was, not a bit like the grim character that she had at first thought him. Had she but known it at the tender age of sixteen, he was just the kind of man she would have been privileged to become engaged to—let alone marry!

How stupid she had been to worry about possible repercussions of the past. As Cathy had said, she needed to get things in the right perspective. Well, she had now. It was odd, though, how she had seen him at the airport the following morning after the restaurant episode, and the woman who had been mentioned, too. He must have been paying a visit to London, as it was obvious that he had been on Totorua for quite some time, so her previous worry had been unnecessary.

It was then that she thought of the remark passed by the lovely brunette at the airport, and some of her complacency left her. She could have been referring to some other incident, yet Cara could not convince herself of this.

She turned restlessly in her chair, no longer drowsy as she thought of the woman who had placed her elegant fingers to her lips to throw him a kiss, and of her own resolution to make light of the unfortunate incident should she ever get the opportunity to talk to the man involved. But how could she have done? How was she to know that he would turn out to be the son of her father's patron?

Her frown deepened as she realised she had missed a golden opportunity. She ought to have mentioned the incident straight away, even though he had not recognised her as the belligerent young girl he had persuaded to return to the village with him six years ago. She sighed; even if she had had her wits about her, it might have been rather embarrassing for both of them, and he had certainly not liked the earlier allusion made by his friends at that dinner party, neither had Cara, come to that. It was better left—besides, she told herself comfortably, he was too sensible a man to let such an incident worry him, and there was no possible chance now of the matter leaking out. The village had been swallowed up by the building of the airport, and although the villagers had been settled further up the roadway, so much had happened in the last six years that there was little chance of anyone recalling what had taken place the day before Cara Vernon was sent back to England.

The one person who would have remembered, and who had been the instigator of the event, Tu-Tu, had since passed on to join his ancestors in greener pastures, for her uncle had written and told her of his death a year ago. The news had made Cara very sad, for in her fond imaginings she had seen herself going to seek him out on her return to Totorua. He had been such a great friend of her father's and would have been happy to learn that she was going to work at the same hospital as her father had.

So there was absolutely nothing to worry about, she told herself happily, and her thoughts turned to lighter matters, such as purchasing some material to make herself some *pareus*. She did not intend to wear conventional dress in her off-duty hours, not in this climate, anyway. Of course, she would have to confine herself to the precincts of the home Pierre Morelon had in mind for her, for it wouldn't do to go wandering around the streets in a *pareu*, as comfortable as the native dress was, since it might cause some speculation, and Cara wanted no such attention drawn to her.

Tomorrow, she mused drowsily, she would take a trip into town to make the necessary purchases for what she termed as her 'coming-home' dress.

CHAPTER FOUR

LATER that day, after her uncle had returned from work, Cara brought him up to date with the recent happenings. The interview, she told him, had not gone exactly as she had expected. 'I'm not too sure of the Matron,' she told him with a rueful grin. 'I'm certain that if I hadn't been able to obtain that reference, she would have found some way of opposing my appointment.'

Her uncle, who had settled himself in his favourite chair and was just glancing through the evening paper, took his attention away from it long enough to nod understandingly. 'Can be very awkward females,' he commented dryly. 'I remember coming up against a veritable dragon in Bart's.' He peered over the top of the paper at Cara and gave her a smile. 'Not that the patients were St Georges by any means, myself included, if you follow my meaning. It seemed to me,' he ruminated slowly, 'that she had sacrificed her life for the good of others, and had just come to the conclusion that the human race wasn't worth it!'

Cara chuckled at his philosophy; he might well have a point there, she thought reflectively. Take Miss Besson, the name of the Matron who had interviewed her. One could not call her a happy person; dedicated maybe, since Cara did not know her well enough to be certain on this point, but she did know a happy person when she saw one, and Miss

Besson did not come under this category—frustrated, was more applicable here, and this was more or less what her uncle had implied about the other Matron.

Uncle Theo resumed his perusal of the paper, and Cara's thoughts roamed on. It was possible, she mused, that the responsibility of the job could get one down at certain times. Perhaps she had had a very tiresome morning before the interview. She sighed inwardly; considering all things, it would be better to withhold judgment. There was time enough to prove her earlier theory, and she hoped she was wrong and would find Matron a gentle, understanding person, and a good friend. In spite of Cara's good intentions this image simply would not jell, and she had a shrewd suspicion it was going to be a case of stepping lightly over what would prove to be very thin ice!

Impatiently she shook these depressing thoughts away, and once again demanded her uncle's attention by telling him of Pierre Morelon's offer of a villa in the vicinity of the hospital, and wasn't it good of him?

With what sounded like a regretful sigh, her uncle put down his paper and gave her his whole attention. 'It's what I thought he would do,' he commented mildly. 'I only met his father once. A good man, and a good friend to your father. I'd say his son takes after him. He didn't have to provide other accommodation for us. If I hadn't already fixed myself up I'm sure he would have seen me settled, too.'

'Oh, I'm sure he would!' agreed Cara enthusiastically. 'He was so understanding about the reference. I felt awful asking him for one, but he didn't

even question it. Just asked his secretary to provide
the necessary.'

She was silent for a few seconds, then seeing that
her uncle was about to lapse into the financial
columns of the paper once more, asked, 'Have you
any idea of where this place is? The place he has in
mind for me, I mean?'

Her uncle frowned, whether from irritation at
being kept from his paper, or whether he was giving the matter some thought, Cara wasn't sure, but
when he spoke it seemed to be the latter. 'It's probably the small place in that courtyard off the boulevard. It's only a stone's throw away from the hospital, if one uses the passageway through the
covered archway.' He coughed delicately. 'Er—I believe it's been empty for some time now. Not that
it's been neglected in any way—I noticed that when
I passed by there a few months ago. Still as pretty as
a country cottage. French architecture, of course,
very pleasing to the eye.'

Cara stared at him in dumbfounded delight, for
she knew the place he was referring to, tucked away
as he had said in a small courtyard off the main
street. Could that be the place Pierre Morelon
meant? Oh, she did hope it was! Why, she couldn't
think of any other place nicer than that one. It had
always caught her imagination, and had given her a
sense of surprise to find such a dwelling tucked
away in the middle of the town's busiest section.

There had been a touch of mystery about it, too,
she recalled as her smooth forehead creased in an
effort of memory. Her brow cleared as she pin-
pointed the occasion when she had asked her father
about the cottage, since its proportions did not war-

rant any other title. Her father, she remembered, had said something vague on the lines of—yes, someone did live there, and had hastily changed the subject, much to the young Cara's disappointment.

Uncle Theo, she thought curiously, had shown the same reluctance to discuss the matter, and remembering his delicate cough, a sign that he was slightly embarrassed, heightened her curiosity. A thought then struck her that made her want to chuckle, and she gave her uncle, now determinedly ensconced behind his paper, a look of wicked amusement. Dear Uncle Theo, without realising it he had given her the clue to the mystery. So that was it! Someone's mistress had occupied it! It was a 'love nest', and had Cara been a few years older when she had first asked about it, she would have been a little quicker off the mark!

In her mind's eye she was standing again in the small passageway off the main street looking through to the courtyard at the villa with its miniature garden. She remembered frothy lace curtains against latticed windowpanes. It had, she thought, a look of unreality about it, and gave you the feeling that if you blinked your eyes or looked away suddenly, the next time you looked it would be gone, the only surprise being that it was still there.

Another thought then presented itself, and this time not such a happy one. If the villa was owned by the Morelon family, and had indeed been used for the purpose suggested by the unwillingness of Cara's menfolk to discuss the matter, then only a member of the family could have put it to such a purpose.

Jean-Paul Morelon! Her brows raised as the answer hit her. It could be no one else, since she plainly remembered her father mentioning once that his patron's family had always had business links in Totorua, but had not resided there until Jean-Paul decided to consolidate all his interests in the island, and had taken up residence there several years before Cara's father had taken the hospital post at Jean-Paul's instigation.

A tiny frown knit her forehead. What had become of whoever it was that had lived there? Had Pierre Morelon given her her marching orders now that his father was dead? No, he would not do that, Cara was sure. Even if he had not approved of the alliance, he would not have been so heartless, and he had been very fond of his father and would not have wanted to go against his wishes. She sighed. The logical answer was that she too had died. Heartbreak perhaps, at losing her lover?

Cara gave herself a mental shake. All this was pure conjecture based on her fertile imagination, and she could be wrong. The sentimental side of Cara's nature hoped that she was not wrong, for in spite of her placid outlook on life, she was a romantic at heart. She could also be wrong, or her uncle could be wrong, in his supposition that she would be offered the villa. At this point a deep chuckle escaped her and made her uncle give her a startled look over the top of his paper. 'Just thought of something funny,' she explained quickly, hoping she could make up a plausible lie to justify her uncle's curiosity if need be, but to her relief he nodded absentmindedly and resumed his reading. Not much of a one for social chatter, was Uncle Theo, and this suited Cara admirably.

On this particular occasion it was a blessing, for had he had any inkling of his wayward niece's thoughts at that time, or indeed of the events that had sparked them off, he would have insisted on some other accommodation being found for her. As it was he would remain in blissful ignorance—as would the man who was being so helpful in getting her other accommodation.

She had been thinking of Cathy's reaction to the news when she heard the full story, and for a split second had envisaged her incredulous reaction to the latest development. The fact that she had had to apply to Pierre Morelon for a reference was startling enough, but add to that highly intriguing situation, the abode to which she had been designated—or could possibly be designated—and you had the makings of an extremely embarrassing mixture.

Her amusement faded swiftly on this last thought. Oh, dear, it wasn't really funny at all. So many complications could arise out of the situation. Her teeth caught her lower lip as the anxious thought that she ought to have made some reference to what had happened all those years ago passed through her mind. Ought she to ask to see him again? Could she somehow idly turn the conversation back to earlier times, something on the lines of, 'Oh, by the way, do you remember dragging a reluctant truant out of the jungle and taking her back to the village?' That was as far as Cara got in her imagination, and it was going to stay in her imagination, for there was no way that she could see of bringing such a scheme to fruition. She would rather forgo the chance of living in the villa than refer to the past, and soon found herself devoutly hoping Pierre

Morelon had other premises in mind for her.

Cara ought to have known better, for two days later the odd feeling she had experienced when she had come face to face with the very person she had earlier hoped to avoid, of some kind of spell that fate had bound around her and Pierre Morelon, revisited her when she received confirmation that she had been allotted the villa.

It was as well for her that she did not have a great deal of time in which to brood on this subject, since the letter she received from Pierre Morelon granting her the lease also told her that it was ready for occupation, and he hoped she would find it a pleasing substitute for her old home. The key, he told her, could be picked up at any time during office hours, as his secretary now had it in her keeping. He ended the letter with a kindly wish that she found her new post an interesting and satisfying occupation.

Some of Cara's earlier doubts dispersed with the letter. He was such a kindly man, she was stupid to worry over possible repercussions—most of which were only in her mind anyway. For all she knew, the villa could have been used to house some old retainer of the Morelons—say a governess, or a housekeeper. She decided not to dwell too much on this theory since she was certain that her earlier deductions had been correct. It did, however, help to alleviate her qualms; in this case ignorance was bliss, and Cara did not intend to seek enlightenment!

Within three days of the date she was due to start her duties at the hospital, Cara had moved what few possessions she owned into the Villa Pépite.

The name of her new home she had found on a small plaque attached to the wall beside the front door, now mostly obscured by a trailing vine that bore a gorgeous purple trumpet-shaped flower, and Cara couldn't have agreed more with the choice of name for such a delightful dwelling. It was exquisite, she thought happily as her eyes roamed over the small sitting-room she was standing in.

Frilled organza curtaining, of the same type that she had seen earlier, protected the privacy of the room, for the sitting room looked out on to the courtyard and small garden fronting the villa. The furniture was feminine without being fussy, or to be more precise, of a feminine taste rather than masculine.

As the villa had been let furnished, Cara did not have any problems regarding furnishings, or having to provide herself with any household article, not even cutlery, for she discovered a canteen of cutlery in one of the kitchen drawers on her initial tour of the villa.

Although small, the villa provided all the necessary requirements for pleasant living conditions. There were two bedrooms, one just large enough to accommodate a double bed, that had, Cara noticed, a silk bedspread of a peach hue. It matched the drapes of a bow-shaped dressing table, which supported a large oval mirror with gilt edging that put Cara in mind of a doll's house she had once seen and admired in the window of a large London store.

The thick lilac carpet and the purple velvet curtains at the window gave her the same feeling of unreality. The room was not unpleasing, yet it had a dreamlike quality about it that made Cara feel like Alice in Wonderland, and she rather expected to meet the White Rabbit round the next corner.

It was not a room she would have felt at home in, and she was grateful that there was a second bedroom. This was more to her taste, although even here the feminine influence was the dominating factor, though not quite so prominent. The single divan was covered with a green and white striped bedspread. The off-white carpeting and the ivory curtains were more to Cara's taste, as was the small unadorned but beautifully grained dressing table. The walls, papered in an embossed eau-de-nil design, and free from embellishment, also received her approval. Yes, this would be her room. It might be a little on the cramped side as far as walking space was concerned, but nevertheless it contained all that she could possibly want.

The bathroom was next to her bedroom, and consisted mainly of soft pink tiling around the walls and on the floor, with the fittings in a black marbled glazing that Cara would have to learn to live with, since there was nothing she could do about it.

The villa almost came under the heading of 'two up and two down', but not quite, for a cosy little dining room had been tucked in between the sitting room and the kitchen, that just lifted it out of that category. Not that Cara was complaining, for it was ideal for her purpose, and just as enchanting inside as the outside had tantalisingly suggested to casual passersby, those that had discovered its existence. Tucked away as it was behind the busy boulevard, it evaded the curious attention it might otherwise have received.

Now that she had unpacked, she had time on her

hands to attend to her correspondence, and decided to write a letter to Ermyntrude, giving her the latest developments, and telling her about the cosy villa she had been so fortunate in obtaining.

When she had finished Ermyntrude's letter, she thought about writing to Cathy, but was not sure just how much to tell her. In the end she decided to only give the details of the interview, and how she had had to obtain another reference from a local person, but did not give names. It would be a long time before Cathy was able to visit her on the promised vacation. She would have to save first, and knowing Cathy, Cara knew this would be no easy task for her, in spite of the good salary she had negotiated from the health farm, that had amazed Cara, and brought an amused chuckle from Cathy. 'Well, you should see what they charge their patients for just one week,' she had said airily. 'They wouldn't even miss what they're paying me.'

Her duty on the correspondence front now done, Cara wondered if she ought to give her uncle a ring to find out how he was settling in at the club. As Pierre Morelon had been so punctual in finding her alternative housing, her uncle had taken it as a delicate hint that they were now ready to carry out the next stage of the airport development. There was no reason, he had told Cara, why he shouldn't move too. It would only be a matter of contacting the club and arranging the collection of his personal effects. Not that he had a lot, since the villa had been leased to Cara's father furnished, as was the villa now leased to Cara.

After ascertaining that all was well that end, and that he was pleased with the room he had been given, she managed to coax an acceptance from him to come and dine with her the following evening, and received an amused, 'They do feed me, you know,' reply.

The next item on Cara's agenda was the making-up of the material she had bought for her *pareus*. She had enough material to make herself three, and being an able needlewoman, envisaged no difficulty in this task. She had found a small enclosed arbour at the back of the villa that provided her with complete privacy, either for sunbathing or for pottering around the small rock garden, that now showed signs of slight neglect, and which Cara would take much pleasure in bringing back to order. It was here that she would be able to wear her chosen dress without arousing comment. This would be her domain; for five days a week she would have to submit to convention, the weekends were hers to do as she pleased. She did not seek companionship, and would welcome the peace her enchanting new home would offer her. She gave a contented sigh at the thought; if her work came up to expectations, she would consider herself a very lucky person.

In this happy frame of mind Cara started to make her *pareus*. It did not take long, for it was more a question of how much material would be needed for each garment, giving herself ample room for movement, and since she was a modest person, making sure that the front piece retained a decorous height that revealed only her bare slim shoulders.

Nevertheless, she thought as she tried the first one on, she could not see herself wearing it in Uncle Theo's presence; the poor lamb would be horrified. She grinned at her thoughts—and if he only knew—she pulled a wry face as she tried the second one on. In many ways her uncle had reminded her of her father, but in this instance there would have been a difference. Her father would have made some wry quip, and even alluded to the past, an incident that would have caused him much amusement. She bit her lower lip as the wetness formed in her eyes. Oh, how she missed him, with his no-nonsense approach to life, and his irrespressible sense of humour that made light of otherwise vexing situations.

It was a pity, she told herself, that she hadn't inherited her father's philosophic views on life. She had a sense of humour, of course, and thank goodness for that, but she was apt to meet her fences before she came to them, as the saying goes. She was also a little on the reserved side, and hated fuss of any kind. In this, she suspected she took after her Uncle Theo, since she could not remember a great deal of her mother.

She was just about to slip off the second *pareu* and try on the third, when a bell pealed from the front of the villa. Cara frowned; it must be the front door bell, yet she was not expecting a visitor. It couldn't, she told herself as she made her way to the door, be Uncle Theo. He was not the sort of person who did anything on impulse, and in any case, he wasn't due until the next evening.

Sheer curiosity as to who her visitor was made her unaware of her apparel, but as she opened the door and met the slightly surprised eyes of Pierre Morelon as he took in her mode of dress, she was made painfully aware of the fact.

Her cheeks flamed pink as she noted the way his

gaze slid lightly over her figure, and his voice was more reserved than it had been when he had last spoken to her. He's embarrassed, she thought wretchedly, and no wonder! How could I have been so thoughtless!

'I was just passing,' he began mildly, 'and thought I would see how you were settling in.'

'Very well, thank you,' Cara managed to stammer out, and wished miserably that she could ask him in, but the chances were that he would refuse—well, he would have to, wouldn't he? she argued silently with herself.

As if aware of her dilemma and deriving, Cara suspected, a certain amount of amusement from it, he said dryly, 'Well, I won't stay. If there's anything you need—anything, that is, in the household line, you know where to find me,' and with an amused nod of the head he made his departure.

Cara stood looking at his tall broad back as he made his way through the courtyard and out on to the boulevard. Just what did he mean by that? she wondered as she slowly went inside the villa again and closed the door.

Anything in the household line, he had said, as if she was likely to ask for anything else. 'Oh, dear,' she muttered softly, 'he must be wondering just what sort of a new tenant he's landed himself with!'

So much for her privacy, she thought sadly; the very first time she had worn the *pareu* since her return and she had had to have a visitor. She shrugged lightly. As least he was not likely to repeat the visit, and it wasn't as if she had had prior warning of the visit, so she couldn't be accused of any ulterior motive in appearing in what the European would describe as a state of half-dress!

The thought considerably cheered her up, and she started planning the meal she would give her uncle the next evening, and made out a list of the provisions she would have to get in.

So the weekend slipped peacefully by, and in no time, it seemed to Cara, Monday was upon her, and armed with the reference provided by Pierre Morelon she presented herself for duty at the hospital.

CHAPTER FIVE

WHEN Cara arrived at the hospital on Monday morning, she made her way straight to the Matron's office, and was about to knock on her door when a pleasant-faced young nurse who was on her way through the corridor told her that Matron had started her rounds.

As Cara was uncertain as to her next step, the little nurse suggested that perhaps she might like to be shown her office, since she must be the new physiotherapist who Matron had said would be starting that morning.

Cara gratefully accepted the offer and was led down the corridor and out across a small covered section towards what looked like an added wing to the hospital.

Eventually they came to an area of the hospital that housed the office staff encompassing records and the appointment desk, and Cara realised that they had arrived back at the front of the hospital.

The nurse had not said much during the journey, but Cara took her silence as shyness, for she understood the Polynesian nature well, it was part of their charm, and when the girl smilingly indicated an office next to the physiotherapy room, Cara thanked her for her help and said that she hoped that she hadn't taken up too much of her time, whereupon the young nurse replied that she was going off duty anyway, but was happy to be of assistance.

The office was small but adequate for her needs, and contained a desk and a chair, and two filing cabinets. Cara sat down in the chair behind the desk and surveyed her domain with a feeling of accomplishment; she had arrived!

A glance at her watch told her that it was a quarter past nine, and she wondered how long the Matron's rounds would take and whether she ought to wander out and introduce herself to some of the people that she would be working with, but on second thoughts decided that she ought to wait for Matron to do the introducing. It would not do for her to step out of line on her first morning, as anxious as she was to start work.

To pass the time, Cara went through the filing system, and found the files woefully short of previous data. It looked as if a big clear-out had been enforced, but no doubt the previous records would be located in the records office should they be required, and Cara hoped that it would not be long before the files were bulging once again with the data of patients' treatment.

By nine-thirty she had explored all her domain, including a peep into the physiotherapy room next to her office and found it well equipped with the necessary aids the exercises required. All she needed now was a list of the patients at present receiving treatment, and she knew that there ought to have been an appointment book about somewhere but had failed to locate it. She must ask about this after she had seen Matron.

On this thought, as if entering on cue, the Matron walked into her office. 'Ah, so you have found

your way here, I see,' she said on a note that
sounded a little peevish to Cara's sensitive ears.

'I hope that was all right,' replied Cara hastily,
thinking that perhaps she ought to have waited in
Matron's office until she had finished the rounds.
'But one of the nurses told me you were on the
rounds and asked if I'd like to see my office. I wasn't
sure how long you would be, you see,' she ended
slowly.

'Oh, that was quite all right,' replied Matron in
a voice that suggested quite the opposite, and hoping to placate her Cara dug in her handbag for
the reference Pierre Morelon had given her, and
handed it to her with a quiet, 'I believe this is what
you wanted.'

It was accepted with an abrupt nod and thrust
into Matron's apron pocket with no accompany-
ing remark, and Cara wondered if she need have
bothered to get it anyway. Either the Matron had
had a bad weekend, or she had not taken to her,
Cara didn't know which, but fervently hoped it was
just the normal Monday morning malady that
seemed to affect all and sundry at one stage or another.

The rest of the morning Cara spent being introduced to various members of staff, a task taken over
by one of Matron's deputies for which Cara
breathed a sigh of relief. She knew Matron was a
very busy person and had no wish to irritate her
further by taking up her valuable time.

The appointment book was finally located in the
physiotherapy room tucked into a drawer of a small
desk used by the assistants delegated to help in the
work, and it was almost midday before Cara could

actually begin to get down to her work, but she was thankful that the initial approach was over and she could now concentrate on the task ahead of her.

There were five new names to be added to her filing system already. These she had been given during consultations with the Sister of each ward she had visited, and who felt that certain patients might benefit from such treatment. On the whole, Cara thought satisfactorily, a very rewarding start to her work.

The following morning, and now wearing a white dress uniform provided by the hospital, together with an impressive-looking badge pinned to her breast pocket that gave her status in gold lettering, Cara waited for her first patient to arrive.

The morning went well and Cara had no complaints about the staff detailed to help her, and found them to be a very competent team.

One member of staff, though, frankly puzzled her, for he seemed to be completely out of place in such work. His burly frame and six foot four height, and dark green overalls such as those worn by the hospital porters, made him look as if he had wandered in by mistake and decided to stay.

A few days later Cara found that her original thoughts on the subject of Armand were correct. He was a porter, and had made himself indispensable to the unit by his willingness to not only fetch and afterwards return the patients to their respective wards, but actually helping in the exercises given to the patients, particularly the less dexterous ones where his strength yet very gentle administration was required.

In the days that followed Cara found that Armand was a tower of strength in more ways than one, for although he was French he had a good command of English, as had most of the nursing staff. This was not the case with the majority of patients, and Armand took on the role of interpreter between Cara and her patients. It said a lot for Armand that none of the nursing staff took exception to this state of affairs; his nature was such that no one could take offence. He was entirely reliable and always lent a sympathetic ear to whatever grievances the young nurses aired from time to time.

The Matron, Cara discovered, was respected but not liked. Even Armand with his easygoing and understanding nature would be sure to side with the nurses on any dispute that involved the Matron, and Cara wondered if he had ever had a confrontation with her, but knowing Matron, Cara simply could not see her lowering her status by entering into any such situation with him. She would be more likely to delegate the task to some other authority. Whatever the cause of his dislike, Cara doubted if she would ever discover it, but it did rather intrigue her, since Armand was not the type of person to harbour a grudge against anyone.

Inevitably she heard scraps of gossip from time to time, and one particular piece gave her a nasty jolt. Her informant on this occasion was Armand, and as such could be relied upon to be absolutely authentic, and it concerned the Matron.

It started with the news that one of the student nurses had been severely reprimanded by Matron for what she termed as 'flagrant disregard of the rules' and the other nurses were discussing the matter. 'She'd got a date,' said one of them indignantly. 'She'd only slipped back to the hospital to give one of the girls a telephone message she'd taken for her at the hostel. As if she'd turn up for duty in high heels and a halterneck dress! She told Matron she was off duty, but it didn't make any difference.'

'Well, it wouldn't, would it?' piped up a young friend of hers. 'If you ask me she's got her knife in Nicola, just as she had with Jan. They were friends, remember.'

This remark prompted another nurse to ask Armand, 'How is Jan, Armand? I haven't seen her around lately.'

Armand shrugged expressively. 'Making out,' he replied tersely. 'Doing office work now. More money in it.'

'A crying shame, I call it,' commented the senior nurse in Cara's team. 'She was a promising student, too.'

'Well, we all tried to dissuade her from leaving,' commented another nurse. 'So did you, didn't you, Armand? But I suppose we'd have felt the same if we were always getting picked on.'

The tight expression on Armand's normally pleasant face told Cara that perhaps she had the answer to Armand's dislike of Matron. Whoever Jan was, it was obvious that he had been very fond of her.

It would not, mused Cara, be a romantic involvement since Armand, at a guess, was in his early fifties, and although there was no hard and fast rule where affairs of the heart were concerned, Cara was sure his feelings were purely altruistic, and it would be in character for him to take a stand against oppression of any kind.

A quick glance at her watch told her that the last three patients would shortly be up from X-ray, and she hoped their arrival would conclude the discussion on past and recent happenings in the hospital. It would not do for any of the remarks to get back to Matron, even though the team conversed in English in deference to Cara, for which she was very grateful since French was their mother tongue but English, too, was a universal language, and there was no guarantee that some of the remarks would not be passed on.

Cara's position at that time was not an enviable one; she was in charge of the team, and as such she ought not to encourage gossip of that nature. To be strictly fair, Matron's role was not an easy one either. You couldn't please everyone, and rules and regulations had to be adhered to.

Fervently hoping that the goodwill that she had so far encountered would not be placed in jeopardy, Cara ventured to suggest that perhaps there was more to the episode than met the eye. To her consternation this was met with instant agreement, though not quite in the manner she had hoped for. Armand looked amused, and the girls looked pleased, leaving Cara with the impression that she had just made a profound statement, but in what connection she had no idea!

She might not have become enlightened had not Armand, who had stayed behind when the morning exercises were over in order to help clear away some of the implements used in the exercises, asked her how she was settling down, and the hostel wasn't too bad, was it?

The assumption that she was staying in the hostel

somewhat surprised Cara, but of course he knew nothing of her circumstances. There had been no occasion before to talk on personal matters, and although she knew it was a kindly enquiry on his part, she also sensed a certain amount of curiosity behind the question.

'I'm not staying at the hostel,' Cara replied. 'I've been very lucky in getting a lease on a villa here.' Seeing the look of surprise this statement produced from Armand, she explained her circumstances, and how the villa she had lived in with her father had been commandeered for the new airport, ending with a bright, 'So Monsieur Morelon offered me the Villa Pépite.'

The name caused Armand to swiftly direct his attention from the walking aid he was just stacking neatly against the wall and give Cara a piercing look. His manner when he next spoke was decidedly on the reserved side, as against his normally friendly approach. 'Are you a friend of Matron's, then?' he asked stiffly.

Surprised, Cara replied hastily, 'No, not really. I hardly know her.'

Armand immediately relaxed his formal attitude and gave her a grin. 'So she didn't get it,' he said half to himself, but Cara heard.

'Is there something I ought to know?' she queried, with a nasty suspicion that she was not going to like the answer.

Instead of replying to this, Armand asked her another question. 'Does Matron know your new address?' he asked with an innocent air as if certain of the answer before she gave it.

Cara took a minute to think this over, and had

to admit that the answer was no. The address given on her original application form had been her previous address and she had not yet altered it. 'No,' she said abruptly, and frowned at Armand. 'You haven't answered my question,' she said accusingly.

He was still not ready to answer, and Cara knew a spurt of frustration at his apparent absorption with his inner thoughts. 'I shouldn't be in too much of a hurry to alter your address,' he advised her with another grin as if savouring some secret amusement from the situation.

'Why?' demanded the now exasperated Cara.

Armand shrugged his burly shoulders. 'Matron's been after that property for the last year or so,' he said slowly, giving Cara a quick speculative look to see how she took the news.

Cara's lovely brown eyes opened wide in surprise, then she exclaimed woefully, 'Oh dear! It could be sticky at that, couldn't it? But how was I to know?' she argued reasonably more for her own benefit than for Armand's. She stared back at him. 'How did you know this?' she asked him curiously, for although she knew there was such a thing as the hospital grapevine where all snippets of news gradually filtered through the ranks, she could not see Matron noising her business abroad.

'Through Jan,' he replied tersely, now on the defensive.

'The girl you were just talking about?' asked Cara. 'The one who used to be a student nurse?'

He nodded abruptly. 'And now works in an office,' he added bitterly, then looked at Cara. 'She's my niece,' he explained. 'And a nicer girl you couldn't wish to meet. Oh, not because she's my sister's daughter. You ask anyone; they all liked her.'

Cara settled herself on the edge of the desk where she had been collecting the notes made on the patients' progress that morning. 'Tell me about her, Armand, and why she left,' she requested quietly.

Armand turned back to continue his work in clearing the area, and Cara had a feeling that he resented her curiosity, though it was more than that for her, and she had a vague suspicion that she was going to wish she hadn't asked. 'I'm sorry, Armand,' she said swiftly. 'It's none of my business, forget it.' She was taking the coward's way out, and she knew it, but what she didn't know couldn't hurt her, could it?

His quick reassuring grin made her spirits sink, for she knew she was going to hear all about it whether she wanted to or not.

'You're in it,' he said slowly, leaving Cara wondering just what he meant by that, then he continued, this time on a more sober note. 'You told me you used to live here before you went back to England,' he said, and giving her another quick look asked, 'What do you know about the villa you've leased?'

Now in no doubt as to where the conversation was leading, Cara flushed a delicate pink, and she debated whether to deny all knowledge concerning the past history of the villa, but her flush gave her away and seeing it Armand gave her an amused look. 'Ah, you English,' he said teasingly. 'We French take such things as a matter of course. So you did know,' he said more as a statement than a question, and Cara could hardly say otherwise, not now.

Still slightly embarrassed, she said almost apologetically, 'Well, let's say I guessed. I wasn't all that old, you know, when I left,' she ended lamely, not knowing what else to say.

'The lady in question,' went on Armand with an air of producing a rabbit out of a hat, 'was Mrs Besson, a retired naval officer's widow.'

Cara just stared at him. Besson! That was Matron's surname! It couldn't have been Matron ... 'Matron's ...' she was about to ask when Armand finished the sentence for her.

'Her mother,' he said blithely.

Cara was extremely glad she was sitting, or at least resting her weight on something. Was that the reason why Matron wanted the villa? she wondered.

As if picking up her trend of thought, Armand gave a swift nod. 'Thinks she's entitled to it,' he said casually. 'Only the new owner doesn't,' he added significantly.

Cara stared down at the polished floor at her feet, seeing not her small neat feet encased in the uniform white brogues, but the face of Pierre Morelon. for it was he that Armand was talking about.

For reasons of her own Cara did not want to pursue the matter, but she did want to know what had happened to the previous tenant. 'What happened to Mrs Besson?' she asked quickly.

Armand looked a little disappointed at the swift change of subject but answered, 'Oh, she died about a year ago. Heart attack.'

Closely watching him, Cara was sure he had a spark of amusement in his eyes, and when he went on to add a few more details she was sure of it. 'It was rumoured that it happened shortly after the reading of Monsieur Morelon's will. Her expectations were not fulfilled, apparently, and she worked herself up to a frenzy.'

Cara's depression deepened and as before she fervently wished she had not asked for these confidences, but she could see no way of stopping her willing informant from giving her the rest of the story.

'It was also rumoured that there had been a difference of opinion,' continued Armand persistently. 'There was another gentleman in the case, a certain colonel that she entertained. And that,' concluded Armand sourly, 'is why Jan didn't stand a chance. Not with the daughter of Mrs Besson, anyway.'

The sudden switch back to the original subject of the conversation threw Cara completely, and she looked as lost as she felt.

'Jan's mother worked for Mrs Besson,' explained Armand. 'What you would call a daily help in England,' he added helpfully, not that this in any way enlightened Cara, who was still lost.

'Mrs Besson was convinced it was Jan's mother who had spilt the beans, as you might say, about the visits of the Colonel. She had been very careful to keep the visits a secret. She was,' he said curtly, 'a very vindictive woman, and made it her business to see that my sister, Jan's mother, did not get another domestic job.' His lips folded tight before he added, 'And she needed the money, too. She was a widow with three children to bring up.'

He was silent for a few seconds before he spoke again and nodded towards the door of the room, 'And she's the same,' he said, meaning presumably the Matron, Cara thought. 'She hounded Jan from the moment she arrived at the hospital for training, and didn't let up until Jan had given her notice in.'

Cara didn't know what to say, although it did strike her that it was hardly credible that someone could carry on a vendetta like that, particularly as the person concerned had died. It seemed so pointless and she ventured to mention this to Armand, but he had the answer to that, too, and one that Cara could not argue with.

'Money,' he said curtly. 'Old Jean-Paul was a very rich man. There was no doubt that if Mrs Besson hadn't decided to burn both ends of the candle she would have been a very wealthy woman after his death. There is also no doubt that the villa would have been hers, too.' He nodded once more towards the door. 'She used to live there with her mother before she went to France for training, and she was expecting to come back to it when she took up her appointment here last year. By that time it was all over. Jean-Paul had died, and her mother shortly after.'

Cara felt a pang of sympathy towards the Matron; in a sense her case had been similar to her own. She too had hoped to return to the home she had known and shared with her only parent. 'How sad for her,' she said quietly. 'It must have been a terrible homecoming for her.'

Armand gave her a surprised look, then shook his head. 'Not sad,' he commented, 'frustrating, yes. She wasn't fond of her mother, if that's what you're thinking. They didn't get on at all. My sister saw enough of them together to vouch for that, and she's not one for idle gossip. Mrs Besson must have known that or she wouldn't have employed her in the first place. It was sheer spite that made her take it out of Marie. The same goes for the daughter, she was expecting to come into a small fortune.'

Cara now had to do some rapid rethinking; but somehow it didn't add up. Matron had not sounded bitter about Monsieur Morelon. In fact she had been just the opposite, even patronising when his name was mentioned. 'I still don't see why Matron should want the villa,' she said perplexedly. 'Unless,' she mused, 'she's in lodgings and wants somewhere to live on her own.'

Armand gave her a pitying look. 'You've met the son, I presume?' he asked sardonically.

Cara frowned, 'Yes,' she replied still mystified. 'But I still don't see ...' Then she did see—most graphically; Pierre Morelon was a very handsome man—he had also inherited the Morelon wealth.

Her eyes widened as the implication hit her, and seeing her expression, Armand nodded in a satisfied way. There was no need of further explanation.

CHAPTER SIX

For the rest of that week Cara felt as though she was living on a cliff edge that any day might crumble under her feet and fling her into an abyss. There was no doubt that Matron would eventually find out that the villa had been let—and to whom!

There was one small crumb of comfort she could derive, though; she had told Matron that Jean-Paul Morelon had been her father's patron, and in view of this, she might accept the situation and not unleash her disappointment on Cara. There was also the reference she had received from Pierre Morelon, and surely this, too, would safeguard her against any comebacks.

On the face of things there was nothing for Cara to worry about, yet she had a niggling feeling at the back of her mind that while Matron might accept Cara's recommendation from Pierre Morelon for a position at the hospital, she would not be so complacent over his leasing the villa to her—particularly as she was the other interested party.

Armand's hints that Matron had a specific goal in mind that had nothing to do with sentiment—at least where her mother was concerned—did not help matters one little bit but decidedly complicated them.

As Cara had not needed further elucidation from Armand on the situation, neither did she need the services of a fortune-teller to give her the end result should things go wrong. Matron's hounding of the nurse Jan would pale into insignificance against the war she would wage against Cara if she thought Cara was moving into what she considered her territory, in other words was developing a romantic *tendresse* for Pierre Morelon!

Had this state of affairs prevailed in England, Cara would have been able to shrug it off as an annoying distraction, but nothing else, and if things did get sticky she would have been able to look for another situation elsewhere. But this was not England, and without a work permit Cara would have to leave the island she thought of as home, and the thought made her more sensitive to the situation than she might otherwise have been. She was in no doubt that should the Matron set her mind to it, she could by various ways and means remove Cara from the hospital.

When thoughts such as these crowded in on her, she found herself wishing that Armand had not been so forthcoming, even though she realised it was his way of forewarning her of possible repercussions once the Matron had learned her new address. There was no point in using delaying tactics either. The sooner she altered her address the better, for if she failed to do this she could be accused of trying to conceal it, and making matters worse than they already were.

Her best ploy, she told herself, was ignorance. She had been away from Totorua for a long time and past gossip would mean nothing to her. It wouldn't have done either, if Armand hadn't made it his business to enlighten her, she thought miserably. Matron would not know this, and should any oblique reference to the villa be made by her, Cara would feign total ignorance on the whole issue.

For two days after she had changed her address everything went as normal, and Cara began to wonder if she hadn't let her imagination get the better of her and the whole thing was just a storm in a teacup. She was on the point of convincing herself of this, when a happening on the third day put her firmly back on the cliff edge again.

It began when a new patient was brought in for treatment by one of the ward nurses, who was about to leave the room when she caught sight of Cara gently manipulating an elderly woman's arm in an effort to try and get some movement out of it.

'Cara Vernon!' she exclaimed in unconcealed delight. 'Remember me, Maaua?'

Cara looked up from her task with the same amount of delighted surprise as shown by the young Polynesian nurse who now held out a slim honey-coloured hand towards her.

Maaua was Tu-Tu's granddaughter, but the fact caused Cara no trepidation at that time, she was only too delighted to find someone she had known and played with during her stay in Totorua. At last she had met someone who could bring her all the news of the village and the playmates she had grown up with.

As it was not possible for the girls to talk there, Cara asked Maaua what lunch break she would be taking and arranged to meet her afterwards in the staff lounge.

The lounge was ideal for the girls' purpose, for at that time of day it was hardly used by other staff and enabled Cara and Maaua to catch up on the news between them without any interruption or interested bystanders.

Many of the girls Cara had known had now married, and two of them had families. Maaua had been the youngest of the group, and Cara thought that she must now be about nineteen years of age, and had grown into quite a beauty, with large, dark honey-coloured eyes that lit up when they spoke of the past.

When all the news in this direction had been exhausted, Cara gave her news, and how she had trained as a physiotherapist, and applied for a job at the hospital.

'We all knew that we'd got a new member of staff,' Maaua said, 'and that she was English, but I never dreamed that it was you. I thought it was terrible for you when you had to leave,' she added sympathetically. 'And I couldn't understand why you had to go.'

'Neither could I,' agreed Cara with a grin. 'Now I'm glad I went. It's not easy to get a job here, you know, and if I hadn't qualified as a physiotherapist, I wouldn't have been able to come back, at least not to stay,' she amended with a smile.

The time flew by and soon they were due to return to their duties. Cara, after finding out that Maaua had a room in the nurses' hostel, invited her to visit her at the villa one evening if she was ever at a loose end. 'It's not far from here,' she told her, 'not if you use the short cut through the archway and that will bring you to the back of the villa.'

It took a moment or so for Maaua to realise what place Cara was referring to and when she did, she gave a deep chuckle and raised her dark eyebrows in query as she asked Cara, 'Do you know who owns that villa?' with just a hint of mischief in her voice.

Cara blinked quickly and felt a tremor of discomfort but managed to answer blandly enough, 'Oh, yes, Monsieur Morelon, of course. His father was my father's patron, you know,' she added for good measure in case Maaua had other ideas on the subject.

Maaua's grin widened, showing a perfect set of gleaming white teeth, and Cara gave her a searching look. She hadn't remembered what had happened the day she was brought back to the village, had she? Even so, she told herself stoutly, she couldn't have known who the man was.

A few minutes later she was asking herself just how wrong she could be. To her utter consternation, Maaua not only recalled the event, but knew the man had been Pierre Morelon!

'For goodness' sake,' pleaded a thoroughly worried Cara, 'don't mention a word of that ridiculous happening. I'd forgotten it,' she lied, 'and so has Monsieur Morelon, so please, Maaua, don't ever mention it again.'

Maaua's lovely eyes widened at Cara's vehemence, and Cara was immediately contrite. She was making mountains out of molehills again. 'I'm sorry, Maaua,' she said quickly. 'It's just that it could make things awkward for me if that story got around the hospital. Not that there was anything in it,' she added casually, and gave Maaua an accusing look. 'Your grandfather must have taken a dislike to poor Pierre Morelon to have attempted to frighten him like that.'

Maaua grinned at this. 'Sure gave us something to talk about,' she said wickedly. 'Place was buzzing with the news for days.'

Cara gave her another searching look, and then grew thoughtful. 'Did Tu-Tu know who he was?' she asked.

Maaua nodded vigorously. 'My granddaddy knew everything,' she said simply.

The news did not surprise Cara one little bit, she had somehow known this. 'Well, I'm glad,' she said airily, trying to shrug off the odd sensation that had once again made itself felt, 'that Monsieur Morelon took it in his stride. He could have made trouble for Tu-Tu, you know.'

Maaua simply shrugged at this, as if it were of no account, then she asked Cara a question. 'Did he recognise you?'

By 'he' she obviously meant Pierre Morelon, and Cara bit her lower lip in vexation; she would rather not have to answer that question at that particular time. 'No, thank goodness,' she got out slowly, adding hastily, 'It would have been too embarrassing for words if he had. So you see why, Maaua, I want it to stay that way.'

Maaua nodded thoughtfully, and realising that Cara was asking for her co-operation in this, assured her with a sober, 'Well, I won't say anything.'

Her reply reassured Cara who thanked her fervently, and reminded her to call in on her one evening, and this Maaua promised to do when her beau of the moment gave her a free evening out.

It was a pity from Cara's point of view that Maaua hadn't been able to resist adding a mischievous rider to their previous conversation. 'Granddaddy was never proved wrong,' she said with a grin just before the girls parted, and Cara's partly amused answer of, 'Well, there's always a first time,' sent Maaua off on her way chuckling, and left Cara gazing thoughtfully after her.

A day later Matron sent for Cara, and Cara, who had been half expecting such a summons, tried to convince herself that it was only natural that Matron should want to know how she was getting on with her work, and that there was no reason to suspect that she had an ulterior motive in asking to see her. However, by the time she knocked on Matron's office door and waited for permission to enter, her knees felt decidedly weak.

One look at Miss Besson's face told Cara that if she did ask her how she was getting on with the work, it would only be a preliminary skirmish to what would most certainly follow.

'Ah, Miss Vernon,' purred Matron in a tone of voice that immediately put Cara in mind of the cat that had swallowed the canary, and now had one paw in the goldfish bowl for the second course, 'how are you getting on?'

Cara swallowed before she answered, 'Fine, thank you, Matron. No problems at all.'

She ought to have added, 'so far', as the look Matron sent her plainly intimated that she was about to change that state of affairs.

'And how are you getting on in your new home?' she asked the apprehensive Cara.

Well, at least she didn't intend to beat about the bush, thought Cara. 'Oh, fine,' was all she could come up with, realising that she must sound like a parrot that had only one word in its repertory, but at least it stopped her from blurting out,' I didn't know you wanted it,' which would have been disastrous, like laying down a dummy hand at bridge and leaving your opponents in full possession of the contents of the hand.

'I'm rather interested in that property myself,' went on Matron conversationally, and then glanced up from the papers she had been glancing at on her desk as if to give the impression that she was only making idle conversation, but she now gave Cara her full attention. 'Just how well do you know Monsieur Morelon?' she asked baldly.

Cara was only too happy to tell the truth. 'Oh, hardly well at all,' she replied as brightly as she was able. 'I thought it was very good of him to offer me alternative housing, but he probably felt responsible—I mean,' she said hastily as she saw the way Matron's eyes had narrowed at this last remark, 'his plans for the airport included our villa— well, not ours, of course,' she amended quickly, feeling she was getting deeper into the quagmire. 'The villa that was leased to us by his father—er—by us, I mean my father and myself.'

'I see,' murmured Matron, in a tone that suggested exactly the opposite. 'The hostel is very well provided for,' she added meaningly.

'I'm sure it is,' Cara agreed hastily, 'but I'm quite happy where I am,' she added foolishly, only seeing a fraction too late that she ought not to have said that.

There was a definite glint in Matron's eyes as she replied tartly, 'Oh, I'm sure you are. However, I feel I ought to warn you that it may only be a temporary residence for you. You see,' she said slowly, giving Cara a sugary smile as if to soften the blow, 'I have a prior claim to the villa that must have been overlooked by Monsieur Morelon, but I'm sure that things will soon be straightened out between us.' Her eyes left Cara and she studied the papers on her desk again. 'My case is somewhat similar to yours,' she remarked in a confiding tone. 'You wouldn't have liked anyone to take over the villa you considered as your home, would you?' she asked Cara.

'No, of course not,' Cara answered swiftly; it was the truth, she would have hated to have come back and found someone else living in her old home.

For this honest answer she received another patronising smile from Matron. 'Very well, then. I take it you have no objection to my telling Monsieur Morelon that you are quite prepared to turn over the lease of the villa in my favour?'

Cara stood looking at her with a slightly stunned expression on her face. How did she get out of that? A moment's reflection told her she didn't, and if the truth were known she didn't want to. She loved the villa and the independence it gave her, but she loved the island more. If Matron got her way, she would have no worries over possible dismissal from the hospital. In a way, it was a thinly disguised blackmail that was being used against her, but she was in no position to argue. 'No objection at all,' she found herself answering steadily.

From then on the interview really did concern work, and no further mention was made about the villa. There was no need anyway, the Matron had got what she had wanted—at least, as far as Cara was concerned, and it was now up to Pierre Morelon to do the rest.

The following week Cara prepared herself for the move that now looked imminent, for she couldn't see even Pierre Morelon withstanding an onslaught from the redoubtable Matron, and even if Cara did not like Miss Besson, she had to concede that she had a prior claim to the villa.

On the Wednesday she received an invitation from Pierre Morelon to attend a cocktail party at his home on the following Friday evening. The invitation did not surprise her, for she saw it as a confirmation that Matron had got the villa, and that Pierre Morelon would use the occasion to tell Cara of his decision to transfer the lease of the villa to Miss Besson. In all probability, Cara mused, he would want to apologise to her for the inconvenience that she would be put to in moving; he was that sort of person.

Later that day she rang up her Uncle Theo to ask him if he had been invited, too, and received an amused, 'No, thank goodness! He used to send me invites to various do's, but it's not my scene, you know. Enjoy yourself, though how, I can't conceive. You won't be able to hear yourself speak, and you'll find yourself jammed in a corner trying to answer two entirely different questions from two equally persistent bores—and doing a conjuring act with a glass of sherry and a plate of those fancy concoctions that are always handed round at such do's,' he chuckled hugely as if already picturing the scene.

After thanking him for his edifying comments on the treat in store for her, Cara hung up with a ghost of a smile on her face. She hadn't told him about the villa, but there would be plenty of time for that later.

Cara chose to wear a white lace cocktail dress for the occasion, and it set off her blue-black hair now twisted into a thick coil on the top of her head. She had also acquired a faint tan by now, and even though she was not one inclined to conceit of any kind, she had to admit to herself that she looked as well as she had ever looked and was quite satisfied with her appearance. So apparently were the un-attached men at the party, two of whom made a beeline for her as soon as she made her appearance. Remembering her uncle's unkind remarks, Cara had to hide a smile when she found herself in just the position he had described, but she was not com-plaining. At least it made her feel part of the oc-casion, for she had been a little nervous of attend-ing such a gathering, and doubted if she would know any of the other guests present.

In this she was wrong, for when a few of the guests who had grouped together over her side of the large beautifully furnished lounge parted to allow a few more standing space, she caught sight of Miss Besson standing talking to a tall slight man whom Cara vaguely remembered seeing somewhere, and this puzzled her until she had the answer; he was one of the doctors at the hospital.

While she answered the questions put to her by her two companions, both of whom were deter-mined to make a start on what they hoped would be a blossoming friendship, she covertly studied Matron. Her fair hair was now long and hung well over bare shapely shoulders, for she had elected to wear an off-the-shoulder dress, and Cara had to admit that the pale blue chiffon three-quarter-length dress highlighted her attractiveness.

It was hard to envisage her now in the stiff uniform of the hospital; she looked an entirely different person, and acted as such, thought Cara, as she saw the way she smiled at her companion even though her thoughts were plainly elsewhere as she would cast several quick looks around her as if seeking someone. The someone would be Pierre Morelon, Cara was sure, and following Matron's last look towards a group of people near the door she caught a glimpse of the tall proud head of their host.

He was so tall that Cara had no difficulty in picking out his progress as he moved amongst his guests. His dark blue suit was elegant without being too official looking, and when he stood before her a short while later Cara noticed how the clear blue of his shirt echoed the colour of his eyes that were now smiling at her as he somehow managed to dismiss the two persistent men who had so far monopolised her company.

'So you got here all right?' he queried, his eyes travelling lightly over her upswept hair style and over her slight figure. Remembering the last time he had given her such a look, Cara felt the colour tinge her cheeks; at least she was presentable now.

'I did wonder if you'd have any trouble securing transport out here, and had half a mind to send a car for you,' he gave her an amused look. 'Your uncle, I've discovered, does not care for these social occasions.'

Cara smiled back at him, 'Er ... no, I'm afraid not,' she answered with a twinkle in her eyes. 'But there was no need for you to provide transport for me. It's not all that far really, is it? I've noticed that there are some people here from the hospital, and I daresay I could have got someone to give me a lift if I'd been stuck,' she added brightly, wondering how Matron would have reacted to that assured statement. Still, she mused, considering the reason why she had been invited, Cara was sure she would have had no hesitation in offering her a lift.

'Yes, there are,' he said abruptly and slightly turned towards a group of people on his left, and Cara following his look, saw that the Matron and her friend were in that group. His brief glance rested on Miss Besson and received a brilliant smile from that lady, who must, thought Cara, have been watching them pretty closely to have been able to have timed such a welcoming response, and would have joined them, Cara was sure, had Pierre given her the slightest encouragement. As it was, he turned his full attention back to Cara, and she caught a look of distaste in his eyes as he asked her how she was getting on in her new job.

Cara would not have described herself as being au fait where matters of the heart were concerned, for she had no experience in these matters. One or two youthful crushes on her good-looking tutors in the past were her sole excursions into the realms of romance, and as these had never got past the dream stage she was hardly qualified to pass an opinion one way or the other. But one did not need experience to see that Pierre Morelon did not care for Miss Besson. There was, of course, Paula, the woman he had left behind, and whom he was probably engaged to, since her rather proprietorial attitude towards him at the airport rather suggested such an alliance. Even so, Cara mused reflectively, being engaged to someone didn't mean you had to dislike other women. But he did dislike Miss Besson, Cara was in no doubt of this, and knew she had not imagined his distaste; it was obvious by the way he had abruptly dismissed not only her smile but her very presence from his mind.

Pierre stayed by her side for the rest of the evening, to the consternation of Cara's other two admirers, and the annoyance of Julia Besson, who had made several unsuccessful forays to join their company, but without seeming impolite, they were always countermanded by an astute move by Pierre, on one excuse or another, 'Would Cara like to see the garden?' being one of them, and even the resourceful Julia Besson finally got the message and retired from the fray.

Under different circumstances, Cara might have been worried, but as it was she only saw Pierre's attentiveness as an extended apology for having to turn her out of the villa, and as she had accepted the situation, she would be able to assure him that she understood completely, and that he had no need to feel apologetic about it.

However, her ready assurance on this matter was never voiced, since the matter was not brought up, and as time slipped by Cara became more and more perplexed. Had he taken it for granted that Miss Besson would inform her of the date she would be taking over the villa? This thought was rejected as soon as it was conceived. Pierre Morelon was not the sort of man to pass such a task on to someone else—but why didn't he say something? By the same token she could not envisage him shaking her by the hand at the close of the evening and casually remarking how much he had enjoyed her company, and by the way, would she mind if Miss Besson took over the villa?

By the end of the evening Cara was beginning to feel slightly desperate, for a horrible thought had taken root in her mind. Supposing Pierre had no intention of allowing Matron to take over the villa? Where did that leave her? She swallowed, she knew very well where it left her—with a one-way ticket back to the U.K.!

Just to add to her misery another unpalatable thought made itself felt. She had told Matron that she hardly knew Pierre Morelon, yet he had made a point of sticking close to her all evening—which would either look as if she had been telling a lie —or much worse, that he had developed a predilection for her company!

It was sheer desperation that made her suddenly blurt out, 'I don't mind Miss Besson taking over the villa, you know. It was her home after all, and I do understand. I'm sure I shall be quite comfortable in one of the hostels. The nurses say they're like hotels.'

Pierre gave her a surprised look as if not quite sure what she was referring to, then his eyes rested briefly on the elegant back of Julia Besson as she made her departure together with several other guests, only stopping to give a stiff-sounding 'Goodnight,' addressed to Pierre, and affording Cara the brief acknowledgement of a very cold look.

'I'll just see the rest of the guests off,' Pierre said quickly, 'then I want to have a word with you.

Don't worry about transport, I'll see you get back to the villa.'

So Cara was forced to wait apprehensively until all the guests had departed. Julia Besson was not going to get the villa, she was now certain of it, and she miserably wondered what she could say to make him change his mind. It was her job that was at stake when all was said and done. In all probability Miss Besson was at this very moment working out ways and means of removing her from the hospital.

One thing did puzzle her, for as far as she could see, there had been no chance of a private conversation between Pierre and Julia—unless it had taken place shortly after she had arrived, and before Cara's appearance. Remembering the way she had smiled at Pierre earlier in the evening, Cara was sure she had not at that time known that her cause was a lost one. Yet she had been in no doubt of the fact by the time she had departed.

Cara's bemused eyes rested briefly on Pierre as he ushered the last lingering guest off the premises, and seeing what a handsome figure he cut, she suddenly had the answer—he hadn't needed to say anything to Julia—his behaviour that evening had given her the answer! She bit her lower lip in anxiety as her racing thoughts ran on. By practically ignoring her, and clamping Cara to his side, he had made his thoughts pretty clear on the issue, but he couldn't have known what the end result was likely to be—for Cara, that was, and as she gave him a tremulous smile in reply to his as he came back to join her, she made up her mind to put him into the picture as soon as possible.

Pierre offered her a drink as he walked towards

the miniature bar at the end of the lounge, and raised his expressive eyebrows at her firm refusal; she had had several sherries, and now wanted a clear head to be able to argue her case.

He fixed himself a small whisky and soda, and brought the glass back with him as he joined her, then pointed to a comfortable-looking deep chair by the ornate fireplace. 'Do sit down,' he urged her gently, 'and don't look so worried. I have no intention of allowing you to go into a hostel. You are to stay where you are.'

Cara took a deep breath. It was now or never! 'I do appreciate your thoughtfulness, but it's not as easy as that,' she began, but that was as far as she got, for Pierre held up an elegant hand to stem her words.

'Please let me finish,' he interjected, still in that gentle almost apologetic voice. 'Firstly, I must apologise for rather presuming on our acquaintance this evening,' and he met Cara's questing brown eyes with a definite twinkle in his blue ones, and she felt a flutter somewhere around the heart region. 'Not that I didn't enjoy every moment of it, I did, but I also had a particular reason for acting as I did.'

Cara had already worked that out for herself, and she knew a slight spurt of annoyance towards this handsome, charming man with cool assurance, and suddenly realised he was more than a match for the Julia Bessons of this world. If he had decided that Cara would stay in the villa, then stay in the villa she would. For how long, though, was questionable—just as long as it took Matron to have her dismissed, she thought miserably. Her depressed gaze lingered on the man now sitting opposite her in an identical chair to hers. His dark head was bent towards the glass in his hand, and although he was looking at the liquid it contained, Cara knew his thoughts were elsewhere.

She felt a spurt of pity for Matron who was certain to lose hands down, not only on her desire to take over the villa, but what she had hoped would be the culmination of such a move. Cara wondered how long Matron had known Pierre. It could have been for years, of course, but there was no doubt that she was in love with him, her every glance had shouted it, even at a distance. There was Paula, too, of course, and Cara was sure that Matron did not know about her, which was a pity— looking at it from a purely personal point of view. If only she had accompanied him back to the island, for with Paula in loving attendance by his side, Cara would have been let off the hook.

'I do feel, however, that I owe you an explanation,' began Pierre slowly, breaking into Cara's musings. 'It's not easy to explain, so I must ask you to bear with me for a while.' He glanced quickly at Cara to note her reaction to what he was about to tell her. 'Did you know or hear anything about the villa during your earlier stay here?' he asked her suddenly.

Cara's cheeks did their party act again, and as with Armand's question, she did not have to answer. He nodded abruptly before carrying on. 'Perhaps what you didn't know was that Miss Besson—er your Matron, that is, is the daughter of the woman who previously lived at the villa.'

It was not easy for Cara to try and assume a surprised countenance, and she was not too sure she succeeded, but she need not have worried, for he did not seem too concerned over her slow reaction at the news. However, when he spoke again she was proved wrong, for he gave her a heartwarming smile, and shook his head as if to clear a fog around his senses. 'Of course,' he said abruptly. 'She would have told you, wouldn't she?' He smiled again. 'She wanted your co-operation, didn't she?'

Cara had to nod in agreement. Co-operation was one way of putting it, she thought wryly.

'She can be a very persuasive woman,' he remarked sardonically, adding on a bitter note, 'as was her mother.'

Now embarrassed, Cara hoped her feelings were not apparent, but once again he correctly interpreted her thoughts. 'I'm sorry,' he said contritely, 'to drag you into the business, but I have a specific reason for not wanting Miss Besson to take up residence there.' He gave a casual shrug of distaste. 'If there were only myself to consider, then people would be welcome to put whatever interpretation they liked on the situation, and Julia Besson would be only too pleased to add to the speculation.' He frowned. 'As it is, the last thing I want is to rake up the past, but I won't bore you with the details now. What I do want is for you to stay exactly where you are. I'm not insensible of the awkward position it will put you in at the hospital, but one thing I can tell you, and that is that should Miss Besson make life difficult for you, you can rely on my assistance to smooth things over for you. I am not without a certain amount of authority there, and I shall not hesitate to use it should the occasion warrant it. You may,' he added, his grim expression relaxing in a smile, 'claim that we were acquainted in the U.K., that should take the sting out of any backlash aimed at you. And now,' he said abruptly, as if it was all settled, 'I'll take you home.'

CHAPTER SEVEN

As Cara prepared herself for bed that night, she wondered if she were really as weak-minded as it appeared. Matron had walked all over her during her last interview at the hospital, and now Pierre Morelon had taken over the reins.

Admittedly there were side issues that slightly complicated things from Cara's point of view, and made it impossible for her to make a stand of any sort. For the first time since her return she almost regretted coming back to Totorua.

Of all the applicants Pierre could have chosen to occupy the villa she was the least suited, she told herself grimly as she climbed into bed and bunched the pillows up under her head. Someone, she thought darkly, must be having a good laugh somewhere at her expense, particularly if there was a hereafter. It wasn't as if she had had a chance to put things right, or at least explain her peculiar position.

As for the reason why Pierre did not want the past resurrected, the answer was, of course, Paula. So he was planning to marry her, at least that had been clarified even if he hadn't actually said so. It was also obvious that they planned to stay on the island, and Pierre was making sure that Matron would not stir up trouble for him in the future.

Cara sighed and reached out a hand to switch off the bedside light, then lay down and tried to lose herself in the arms of Morpheus, but either Morpheus had deserted his post, or her brain refused to comply with his soothing remedy of sleep, for she lay wide-eyed and alert as her mind went on turning over the events of the evening.

It was all very well, she thought crossly, for him to assure her that she had only to ask for his help and all her troubles would be resolved. What did he know of hospital life? It was a world within a world, and if one compared it to a ship, then Julia as Matron was captain of that ship. How she was expected to run to him for help in whatever vexing situation befell her, she couldn't imagine. They might only be slight irritations, but in the end such irritations could become unbearable—more like a war of nerves—a tactic that Julia would be quite adept at, Cara was sure.

His suggestion that she should claim previous association with him was a non-starter too, as she had already outlined her position on this with Julia. She saw no point in telling Pierre this, it was too late now to do anything about it.

She sighed once again and turned over and thumped her pillows hard as if it were their fault that she couldn't get off to sleep. The irony of it all, she thought grimly, was that none of these things would matter if it hadn't been for one certain event in the past. It was not as if she hadn't tried to tell Pierre about it, but whenever she made the attempt she was forestalled, almost as if certain forces were ranged against her, binding her tongue and effectively preventing any such communication

If there were such a thing as a hoodoo, then Cara might as well give in whatever the outcome, she was too firmly enmeshed in the net that had been so insidiously flung over her, and like the fish caught by the tide, had to give up the struggle and await the inevitable. On this thought she fell asleep, lulled by the sound of waves breaking on the reef, a sound that was only in her mind, yet could be heard as plainly as if she were standing on the sea shore.

The following week was an exhausting one for her, mainly because she expected another summons from Matron, and was on constant lookout for trouble in any direction. The fact that no such summons was received only heightened the tension Cara felt gathering around her. There were the small odd pinpricks, that could have been put down to normal happenings such as having her most competent nurse transferred to Medical, and having to accept a replacement who looked and acted more like a wardress in an open prison than a nursing Sister.

It came as no surprise to find that Sister Dufour, the name of the hard-faced and glint-eyed replacement, was a particular friend of Julia Besson's and as such her arrival coincided with a complete change of atmosphere in Physiotherapy. No longer did the girls chat amicably together but they were very careful in what they said, and the conversation was confined to medical jargon.

As the woman held the rank of Sister it made things doubly hard for Cara, for it was obvious from the very first day she arrived to take up her new duties that Armand was not going to submit to her authority. His expressive look at Cara that plainly said, 'I told you so', and the way his normally pleasant face hardened when he glanced towards Sister Dufour, spelt trouble with a capital T.

If Sister Dufour spoke English, she declined to use it, but by now Cara had managed to polish up her knowledge of French, and blessed the fact that she had had an extremely good grounding by her former tutor during her earlier years on the island. Hearing the language day by day had reawakened the dormant teachings and she was now able to understand most of what was said.

Thus she was able to hastily intervene when the first altercation between Sister Dufour and Armand took place. Cara was not able to witness the start of the quarrel, or what had caused it, since she had slipped into her office a few minutes earlier to collect a file on one of the patients, but she was in time to hear Sister Dufour threaten to have Armand removed from Physiotherapy and returned to what should have been his work, merely portering, adding with an acid rider that she couldn't think why he was being retained in that department.

Cara jumped in on Armand's side. She might be able to understand French, but as yet she was not competent enough to express her feelings on the matter in that language, so she spoke in English.

There was no doubt by the flash of temper in Sister Dufour's eyes that she perfectly understood what Cara was saying, and she pursed her thin lips tight when Cara said that Armand's services in that department were invaluable. Trying to soften the words that had sounded as furious as she felt, mainly through dislike of the woman, Cara added a light rider to the effect that she did hope Sister Dufour would settle down in the department. It was early days yet, she knew, but she was sure that given time, Sister would find Armand's assistance as valuable as the other nurses had found it.

Unfortunately, Armand's expression did nothing to confirm Cara's hopes in this direction, if anything it seemed as if he would be quite content to receive his marching orders—at least it would put him out of a certain person's vicinity!

Small pinpricks they might be, but what a world of difference they made to Cara's working day. Also, it had not escaped Cara's attention that Sister Dufour's presence had another purpose—apart from disrupting the normally happy atmosphere in Physiotherapy—and that was to watch points on all issues and report back to Matron; in other words, she was Matron's spy. How she was expected to run to Pierre for help in these circumstances was beyond Cara's comprehension. There would be nothing he could do about it, as she had thought at the time he had made the offer.

Pierre, it appeared, was not the only one who could make his feelings plain without a word spoken, since Matron had undoubtedly chosen to use the same tactics on Cara. Although it was unpleasant, Cara preferred this method to another interview with her, particularly as she was in such a vulnerable position.

No matter how one looked at it, it was not an ideal situation, but Cara was forced to make the best of it. All she could hope for was that in time things would settle down, and that eventually Matron would concede defeat. On this thought she gave a long drawn out sigh for try as she might, she could not see this happening. If it was only the villa Matron wanted, then there might have been a good chance of such a happening coming to pass, but there was Pierre—and Pierre loved Paula. Cara's frown cleared as a thought struck her; she had forgotten Paula—if only Paula would appear on the scene! She had to put in an appearance some time, surely? and the sooner the better from Cara's point of view. All she had to do, she told herself, was to carry on as normal and not give Sister Dufour any opportunity or cause for complaint against her, and who knew, she told herself cheerfully, she just might end up as Matron's best friend, particularly if she thought that Cara also had designs on Pierre!

Cara's hopes that her uncomfortable position would shortly be alleviated were soon to be realised, but not quite in the manner she had envisaged. Had she been given the choice she would have chosen a less painful release from the situation. However, like everything else that had happened to her since her return to the island, she had to accept what fate had in store for her.

It was a visit of Maaua's to Physiotherapy that began the turn of events that led to the culmination of all that Cara had feared would happen should a certain piece of information be divulged and reach the ears of the Matron. At the time of the visit, however, no such worry had impinged upon Cara's consciousness, and she gave a welcoming smile when she saw who her visitor was. On learning that Maaua had called to find out if it would be convenient for her to visit Cara that evening, Cara assured her that it was, adding in a pleased tone, 'Come as early as you can, I'll fix a meal for us.'

Sister Dufour, who had viewed Maaua's visit with avid curiosity, remarked afterwards to Cara that she thought the junior staff were a little too familiar for their own good, and hinted that Cara ought not to encourage them.

Cara was too surprised to feel angry at her comments. 'I invited her to visit me,' she said calmly, and added swiftly on seeing the Sister's lips thin in disapproval, 'Maaua's an old friend of mine, I used to play with her when I was younger.'

As she watched the surprised expression this statement produced on the Sister's usually set features, she felt a spurt of gratification. If she hadn't known before that she used to live on Totorua, she knew now, Cara thought a little maliciously, but later chided herself for her uncharitable attitude towards the Sister, and wished she could find something likeable about her. Unfortunately there was not much to like about a person who set out to make trouble for those around her, and as charitable as Cara tried to be, she could not condone such patent mischiefmaking.

Maaua arrived shortly after six and Cara, who had prepared a Caribbean-style salad for them, added a few anchovies to the final dish as she chatted to her. There had not been much time for her to get in all the ingredients necessary for the spicy salad, there were no red peppers for instance, or olives, but she had managed to produce a passable concoction, even to the extent of garnishing the top of the salad with several dollops of a red jelly that she had made the previous evening and had intended to use as a sweet for her evening meal.

As might be expected, the conversation centred

around their work at the hospital, and Maaua was just as curious about Sister Dufour's presence in Physiotherapy as the Sister had been about her visit. 'What was she doing in your department?' she asked Cara.

Cara's smile slowly faded on the change of subject, since they had been discussing more pleasant aspects of hospital life. 'Oh, she's joined us.' she said casually, but her depression was echoed in her eyes.

'Poor Cara!' sympathised Maaua. 'She's not the most popular Sister in the hospital. It's odd, though,' she mused, 'she's been with Medical for years,' then she gave a light shrug. 'Perhaps she wanted a change,' she suggested, but did not sound too convinced of this.

'Perhaps Matron wanted her to change.' Cara commented dryly. 'I understand they're friends.'

Maaua looked up from her absorption with her food, and her finely arched brows rose a fraction higher as she asked, 'You haven't upset Matron, have you, Cara?'

Cara shook her head, and handed Maaua the basket of bread. 'Of course not!' she answered, and before she had thought of where her next question would eventually lead them, she asked, 'How well does Matron know Pierre Morelon?'

Maaua selected a piece of bread and put the basket down on the table before answering, and Cara knew she was seeking the reason as to why such a question should have been put to her. In the end she gave it up, and with another light shrug of her slim shoulders she replied, 'Well, I suppose they used to see something of each other when they were young. Tennis clubs and things like that.'

She gave Cara a considering look. 'I only know what I've been told, you know. I shouldn't have thought they were friends—well, not as you and I are friends, I mean, just acquaintances, I would say. I expect they meet at all the parties and things that are going on. Most of the doctors receive an invitation for them, and she would make sure she accompanied one of them, particularly if it was one of Pierre Morelon's parties. Everyone knows she's got a thing about him.'

There was a few seconds' silence while the girls tucked into their meal, then Maaua, who was still trying to work out Cara's interest in Matron's love life, suddenly felt she had the answer. 'Of course,' she murmured brightly, 'you wouldn't know much of the past history, would you? I wouldn't have known either, except that I came to work at the hospital, and you know how gossip can fly around there. Matron's only been at the hospital a year, you know, she trained in France, and came back here as Matron. I wouldn't say it was a popular choice—oh, she's qualified all right, but she has a way of putting people's backs up, but it doesn't seem to worry her; if it did, she would do something about it and try to be a bit more understanding. She has a way of looking at you and making you feel small.'

Cara nodded her agreement with this observation. She knew exactly what Maaua meant, and it was some comfort to know that she was not alone in receiving such treatment. 'She didn't take too kindly to my living here,' she said dryly, 'apparently she was after the place, too.'

Maaua's eyes opened wide at this. 'So she's after your blood!' she exclaimed.

Cara's eyes went to the bright salad bowl in the centre of the table before she answered slowly, 'To be honest, I'm not really sure about that. All I know is she did try to get Pierre Morelon to change his mind about leasing me the villa, and to lease it to her.'

'But she didn't succeed,' interjected Maaua softly. 'Well, she wouldn't, would she? It was her mother who used to live here—rent free, if you know what I mean, and he wouldn't want the past raked up again. His mother went back to France. Pierre Morelon used to spend his holidays here with his father, and the rest of the time with his mother.'

As Cara recalled the look of sorrow Pierre had given when speaking of his father, she thought that he must have had a sad childhood, since it was obvious that he had been fond of both his parents. 'No,' she agreed emphatically, answering Maaua's first observations, 'he wouldn't be likely to want the past resurrected. But it puts me right in the middle, doesn't it?'

'Right in the middle,' agreed Maaua, and gave Cara an impish grin, but then sobered as she reviewed the situation. 'It's rumoured that she hoped to do better than her mother, where the son was concerned, I mean,' she observed thoughtfully. 'Jean Paul Morelon never married her mother, and he could have done, you know. He was a widower for several years before he died, but there was some row, I think, and he lost interest.' She turned a sympathetic eye on Cara. 'So she's taking it out on you.'

'It does appear so,' Cara said quietly, 'and it didn't help matters when Pierre Morelon invited me to a cocktail party the other evening and insisted on keeping me company,' she added gloomily.

Maaua digested this news for a moment or so before giving Cara another mischievous smile. 'So my granddaddy was right after all, wasn't he?' she teased Cara.

Cara laid down her knife and fork with a dull thud on to the table and gave her an exasperated look. 'I thought we'd agreed not to mention that,' she answered crossly. 'And considering Pierre is practically engaged to a girl named Paula, I'm afraid Tu-Tu was way off the mark.'

'Does Matron know about this Paula?' asked Maaua curiously.

Cara shook her head. 'I don't think so—no, I'm sure she doesn't. I only wish she did, it might take a little of the pressure off me. I'm sure she thinks I've got my eye on her Pierre, and I haven't,' she said, firmly meeting the twinkle in Maaua's eyes. 'I'll admit he's nice,' she conceded grandly, 'but I'm not poaching on anybody else's preserves, intentionally or unintentionally, and,' she added dryly, 'it's not as if he were interested in me, not in that way anyway, so you can take that smug look off your face,' she advised the now chuckling Maaua.

When Maaua was brought back to sobriety, she agreed with Cara that the appearance of the woman Pierre Morelon was in love with would certainly ease things for Cara, and in the meantime she advised Cara to watch her step and not give Matron any cause for complaint against her.

The following week the storm Cara had sensed was gathering around her broke out with a ferocity that left her completely defenceless on all counts, for even her staunch ally Pierre Morelon joined the forces ranged against her.

It began with another invitation from Pierre, to yet another cocktail party, and at first Cara was tempted to plead another engagement, but as she knew so few people on the island, apart from the staff at the hospital, she was afraid he might take her refusal as a snub of some kind, and she had no wish to offend him.

The reason for the invite, she was sure, was that he wished to satisfy himself that all was well her end, and that was going to be the tricky part. To just report the bare facts as they stood would not mean a thing to him. Personnel were often moved around in a hospital and the fact that the replacement sent to her department was a special friend of Matron's would have no significance for him.

On the other hand, to say that all was well would be a downright lie, and all Cara could hope was that no such query was put to her, since there was nothing he could do about it, even if he understood the position she was in. All these thoughts went through her mind as she got ready for the party, and as she fastened the wide velvet belt of her wine-coloured dress around her slim waist, she fervently wished she might get the opportunity of a word with Julia Besson at some time during the evening.

It all depended, she told herself pessimistically as she swept her blue-black hair into a french pleat, on whether Pierre gave a repeat performance of the last showing, or whether he left her room to manoeuvre. Somehow she had to convey the news of Paula's existence to her. It would only need a few simple words if Julia should make any oblique reference to Cara's friendship with Pierre.

She had just picked up her evening bag when the taxi she had hired to take her out to the imposing Morelon residence situated in a prominent position on the hillside overlooking the harbour hooted outside her villa.

By the time she arrived at her destination, and made arrangements for the taxi to pick her up later, her nerves were as taut as a violin string. She would not get another opportunity like this, come rain or shine she was determined to clear the air as far as Matron was concerned. It would not be a pleasant showdown by any means, and Cara suspected Matron was just as keen to have a private word with her, but for slightly different reasons. The very fact that Cara had managed to survive under the eagle eye of Sister Dufour must have aggravated her considerably. In all probability she had hoped that Cara would seek an interview with her and want to know why her nurse had been transferred to another department when she had been perfectly happy where she was. Had it been any other hospital, Cara would undoubtedly have done this, but in her precarious position it was a case of the survival of the fittest, and she knew better than to force an issue on the matter.

As she entered the wide cool hallway of the elegant villa built in the Spanish style, she was too intent on her thoughts to notice or admire the beautiful arrangement of flowers banked on either side of the inlaid glass partitioned door that led directly into the spacious lounge.

The noise of chatter and clinking of glasses told

her the party was well under way even though it was only eight-thirty. As her entrance had not as yet been observed, she took the opportunity of ascertaining that Matron was present, but when her first glance round the room failed to locate her presence, Cara had a nasty suspicion that perhaps this was one occasion that she would not be attending—or worse still, that she had been excluded from, and if this was so, then Cara might as well go straight back to the villa and start packing—since there was no possibility of Matron not knowing about the party. News travelled fast on the island, particularly party news.

At this point Cara found herself wondering whether Cathy needed any assistance on the health farm back home, but then she caught sight of her quarry as a rather tall man stepped to one side to place a glass on a tray carried by an attendant waiter.

Pierre, too, came into her vision at this point and when her eyes lighted on the woman standing by his side, Cara felt a flow of relief wash over her. It was Paula, she was absolutely sure, even though she now had a different hair-style from the one she had worn when Cara had first seen her at the airport, but there was no mistaking that lovely, if slightly haughty, face.

Her relief was followed by a surge of happiness. She had no need to seek out Matron now, and her face broke into a radiant smile at the thought of her reprieve from this unpleasant task. It was at this point that she met Pierre's eyes as he glanced around the company and then made his way towards her.

'I've been keeping an eye out for you,' he said airily, his smile echoing Cara's. 'You've not been here long, have you?' he asked kindly.

Cara answered in the same carefree tone, 'No, I've only just arrived.'

He nodded his dark head as if pleased, then gently caught her arm by the elbow and guided her across the room to where Paula stood. 'Come and meet a friend of mine,' he said, as they joined the lovely dark woman whose eyes had never left Pierre's tall figure as he had gone to greet Cara.

'Paula, I want you to meet Cara Vernon, she's what you might call an old family friend,' and turning to Cara who held out a welcoming hand towards Paula, 'Cara, this is Paula Ericson, another refugee from the U.K. who's just stopped off for a few weeks to get herself a tan.'

Paula's lovely violet eyes, that put Cara in mind of a pansy, opened wide at this jocular statement. 'Not only a tan, darling,' she murmured throatily in a manner that made Cara feel slightly de trop and not a little embarrassed.

Cara took due note of the fact that Pierre had not said anything about Paula being a well-known personage, and she wasn't sure whether she ought to mention this when she spoke to her, but on second thoughts decided to follow Pierre's lead and say nothing on those lines. For all she knew Paula might not wish to make the fact known—that way, she would be assured of some privacy.

'Cara's only just out from the U.K. too, Paula,' Pierre remarked as he smiled at Cara, 'and I trust is settling down well?'

Cara returned the smile, taking care to include

Paula as well. 'Oh, well I do know Totorua, remember, but yes, everything's fine, thank you.' She meant every word; it no longer bothered her that Julia Besson's eagle eyes were upon her, for she could feel them boring into her even though she stood halfway across the room from her.

In singling her out for an introduction to his Paula, Cara knew Pierre was firing another broadside in her defence and was out to spike Julia's guns. Had it been anyone else but Paula, this preferential treatment might have caused Cara a lot of concern, but now that she was present, Cara had no worries at all, and knew a surge of grateful warmth towards Pierre for his thoughtfulness.

For a brief interval she found herself chatting to Paula while Pierre circled his guests, and as they made polite conversation, Cara surreptitiously studied the other woman. Her off-white gown of a chiffon-like material was deceptively simple, much like the woman herself, mused Cara as she noted the way her wide eyes only rested on her for a brief second before they drifted away across the room again, presumably in search of Pierre's tall back.

Although Paula was very gracious to Cara, Cara was not too sure she liked her manner. It hinted at patronage, but Cara shrugged this thought aside. Paula had every right to behave as she did, for she had the world at her feet—even Pierre, and at this thought Cara felt a shadow touch her new-found happiness and gave an inward sigh. Did she realise just how lucky she was? wondered Cara. All that talent, combined with beauty—of course her success would be assured, the combination demanded it.

It was a relief for Cara when Pierre came back to join them, as it meant that she could now drift away and mingle with the other guests. A relief shared by Julia, Cara was certain, for she had had Cara in her sights for some time now, and would jump at the opportunity of a word with her, if that was the right definition for the purpose she had in mind, Cara thought with an inward smile.

Her plans, however, of mingling with other guests came slightly adrift, for Pierre seemed determined to thwart any such move, and an exasperated Cara had to accept the situation. For someone who wanted to help her, he was being extremely unco-operative, she thought glumly, since there was more than an outside chance that Paula would soon be joining Julia in the dislike campaign against her. Men could be so thoughtless at times, Cara thought crossly, for in spite of Paula's slightly off-hand acceptance of her company, it was obvious that she wished her elsewhere, and Cara would have been only too happy to oblige her.

There was only one recourse left to Cara and she took it by excusing herself from their company and making her way to the powder room, not failing to note Paula's swift and relieved-sounding, 'Of course,' at Cara's removal from the scene.

Her suspicion that Julia would seize the opportunity of a word with her was proved by her arrival in the powder room shortly afterwards, only biding her time to talk to her while she waited for the only other occupant of the room to finish her toilet.

Cara took her time in applying the touch-up to

her lipstick, and making sure her hair was behaving itself and no stray tendrils had escaped from the style she had chosen, while Julia stood beside her intent on the same purpose, but Cara knew by the tight expression on her face that as soon as the door had closed behind the elderly woman who was just about to leave, she would give vent to her feelings.

'So you hardly knew Monsieur Morelon?' Julia spat out at her as the door shut with a click behind the woman.

Cara met her furious eyes in the mirror. 'I've not lied to you,' she answered calmly. 'I told you that his father was my father's patron, and as such, he regards me as a friend.'

Julia gave an unladylike snort at this. 'Oh, yes, I admit you've been extremely clever over that bit of it. As to regarding you as a friend—well, that's one way of putting it,' she bit out. 'He's keeping you, isn't he?'

Cara's surprise showed in her eyes as she studied the glinting ones of Julia, then her glance moved on to take in her flushed cheeks. There was no doubt about it, she was incensed about something, so incensed she was not thinking clearly or she wouldn't have made such a stupid accusation. It was so stupid that Cara did not stop to analyse why such an accusation had been made, and decided to ignore it. 'I fail to see why you should be so interested in my friendship with Monsieur Morelon,' she said calmly, willing herself not to lose her temper.

'Don't act the innocent with me,' ground out Julia, 'I heard a very interesting story the other day that explained quite a lot of things. Why you got the villa, for one thing. I suppose you're hoping for a civilised ceremony eventually, but if he's anything like his father, he won't be that easy to tie down. I only hope,' she spat out, hardly able to contain her fury, 'that you get the same treatment as my mother—left without a penny!'

Under her slight tan Cara's face went white; either Julia had lost her senses or she did know something about the past, and Cara was very much afraid it was the latter. She seemed very sure of her facts—sure enough to accuse Cara of being Pierre's mistress, only here her imagination had soared beyond the realms of fact and jealousy had coloured her thinking processes. Cara tried to reason out how Julia had come by the knowledge of what had taken place between Pierre and herself six years ago, since she could not see Maaua breaking her promise to her. There must have been someone else working at the hospital who had come from the village, and it could have been anyone; there were many locals employed in various capacities there.

In a sense Cara was glad it was out, and it was now up to her to bring the incident into proper perspective. She managed to inject a jocular note into her voice. 'What a lot of fuss over nothing! I fail to see why such a ridiculous incident should cause you so much speculation. I can assure you that neither Pierre Morelon or myself attached any importance to it then or now,' she added, meeting Julia's eyes firmly, as if warning her not to make a issue of it.

'I'm sure that Monsieur Morelon would have wanted things that way,' Julia said suggestively, totally ignoring Cara's warning eyes, 'but that wouldn't have suited you, would it? I'd say you'd timed your reappearance here quite nicely. Pierre Morelon's now a very rich man and under the circumstances he hadn't much option but to offer you the villa.'

Cara gave a quick gasp of amazement. It was bad enough being accused of being Pierre's mistress, but to suggest that she was blackmailing him as well was more than she was prepared to take. 'I would take another look at the facts,' she advised Julia coldly, now as furious as her opponent, 'and you'll find that there's absolutely no evidence to support your outrageous accusation.'

She took a deep breath in order to calm herself down, for she wanted to scream and shout at this woman who had harboured such vindictive thoughts about her simply because she had lost out on a private scheme of her own. 'The decision to lease the villa to me was taken by Monsieur Morelon, and was not due to any pressure on my part, but as a gesture of friendship between his family and mine. If you still don't believe me, do you think he would have invited me here tonight to meet his fiancée if there was a grain of truth in what you've insinuated? Of course he wouldn't!' she added scornfully.

There was no doubt that Julia had received a shock, and for a moment Cara felt sorry for her, but there was no other way she could prove her point.

'That must have been quite a shock for you,' spat out Julia spitefully, only just managing to control her feelings. 'I can't see her taking second place, she looks as if she knows her way around. No wonder

he made a point of keeping you with them all evening—he couldn't take the risk of you letting something slip, could he?'

Cara stared at her in fascinated curiosity. She
really believed what she was saying, she thought.
It was as if she were reasoning it all out in her
mind and had spoken her thoughts aloud, much
as Cara was apt to do herself. So much for her
earlier attempts to straighten things out! It was
useless to try and get through such determined
reasoning, and Cara was too weary to try. 'Have
it your way, then,' she said quietly, and on these
words she left the fuming Julia to vent her last
fusillade at the empty room, and made her way
back to the party.

CHAPTER EIGHT

CARA did not stay long at the party after her shattering encounter with Julia Besson, and begged a lift back to town from an elderly couple she had met at the previous party. Her excuse of a headache was a true one, for her head was buzzing with the unpleasant implications that had been levelled at her.

Even though she knew that Julia's outburst had been born out of spite and sheer unhappiness, it did not lessen her distaste of the situation that she had unwittingly landed in.

As soon as she arrived back at the villa, she closed the door behind her with a grateful sigh and leant against the solid woodwork. The little villa seemed to welcome her back and as she gazed at the dainty occasional table in the hall that accommodated the telephone, beside which she had placed a bowl of sweet-scented frangipani of a delicate primrose colour, her eyes misted over.

The villa, like the island, had held out so much promise of happiness to her, yet none of it had come about. From the very moment she had stepped off the plane she had been made to follow a pattern of seemingly predestined moves. At no time had she been allowed to sit back and savour what she had dreamed would be her triumphant return to the island she thought of as home. It was as if the fates were in a hurry to get something over with and were pushing her towards the culmination of whatever they had in store for her. Ought she to have stayed in England, was she not wanted here? Cara shook her head bewilderedly; she didn't know the answer, so it was no use dwelling on such morbid thoughts. In all probability, she told herself stoutly, she was suffering from shock, for Julia had shocked her. Cara had never harboured hate or vindictive thoughts against anyone in her life, although she had come very close to it when Pierre had forced her out of her hiding place shortly after her father had died.

Pierre! Cara suddenly blinked as his name entered her consciousness. She must talk to him! He had to know about the rumour that would shortly be circulating the island fanned by the avenging Julia, for only he would know how to deal with it.

Cara chewed her bottom lip in anxiety as she looked at her watch. There was no chance of a private talk with him that evening, his guests would still be present and would not start to leave for at least another hour. With a sigh she acknowledged the fact that there was nothing she could do that evening, and would have to leave the problem to look after itself until the following evening. A tiny prick of pain told her she had pierced her soft lower lip in her anxious worry. How was she going to get Pierre to visit her at the villa—what excuse could she make for such a visit, particularly as Paula was there—in all probability staying at Pierre's home—and what if he brought her with him! Cara swallowed on this thought; explaining things to Pierre was embarrassing enough, but to have Paula standing by his side while she did so was too painful to envisage.

In fact the more she thought about it the more panic-stricken she became. How does one start such a conversation? 'Oh, by the way, if you hear any rumour about my being your mistress don't take any notice of it, it's just Julia Besson's way of trying to make trouble for you.' Her nails dug into her palm as she envisaged the reaction this calm statement would evoke—how can one be casual about a thing like that? She couldn't—no more than she could see herself calmly discussing the matter.

Her frantic mind explored other possibilities, such as sitting tight and saying nothing, but she couldn't in all fairness do that. She owed Pierre some allegiance, and forewarned was forearmed, particularly as Paula was there. Julia couldn't have picked a better time for stirring up trouble, she thought miserably, since Pierre would now have the worry of the rumour reaching Paula's ears and this, Cara thought shrewdly, would suit Julia's purpose admirably. In a way it was her fault, Cara reminded herself miserably; if she hadn't taken it upon herself to put her in the picture, Julia would have confined her vindictive attack to Cara. Now however, thanks to a self-preserving action of hers, Julia had two targets to aim at. It all depended on how much Paula loved Pierre, and whether she allowed a spiteful woman to break up the romance. Even if Julia did not succeed, she would have planted the seeds of suspicion, and facts were facts, Cara conceded unhappily. Pierre had arranged for Cara to live in the villa—though it was doubtful if he would have done if she had only mentioned a certain incident to him—so it all came back to her and what was really gross negligence on her part— she hadn't given Pierre a chance!

She would write to him! The thought brightened her outlook for a moment or so; it would be less embarrassing for them both if she did that. She could drop the letter in at his office the following day—she could even explain why she had not mentioned the incident that had given rise to so much speculation, say that in her opinion it hadn't been of any significance, and she was sure that he would have been of the same opinion. And he would have been, she whispered fiercely to herself, if it hadn't been for a certain person's intervention!

Oh, it was no good! Even if she took the trouble to write to him, he would still have to see her and discuss the best way to handle the situation, as embarrassing as it was, there was no other way.

Tomorrow perhaps she would see things differently, be able to come up with a few ideas herself maybe, but she was too tired then to cope with the startling turn of events. She would go to bed and hope that she would be able to sleep, although she very much doubted this, but there was little else she could do at that late hour.

It wasn't until she was setting her alarm clock that she realised that the following day was a Saturday, and the start of a long weekend, for Monday was a public holiday, but there was no relief in this thought either, for it might prove more difficult to contact Pierre since he would most probably be entertaining his guest at home—and in that case, Cara would have to wait until the Tuesday to contact him at the office, since she had no intention of spoiling his weekend, particularly as Paula was there.

Contrary to expectation, Cara fell asleep as soon as her head touched the pillows. Her sleep was quite peaceful, and would have been quite exhilarating had she not had to face up again to her troubles the moment she awoke the following morning.

For most of the next day, she pottered around the villa finding various odd jobs to do inside, and also outside on the small rockery at the back of the property, pulling out what looked like weeds, although she couldn't be absolutely sure that they were, but it helped her to keep her mind off her worries for a short time at least.

For a while she toyed with the idea of asking her uncle to share her evening meal, but some inner caution warned her to leave the evening free, and although she was inclined to put this vague uneasy feeling down to nervous reaction, she nevertheless obeyed her inner instinct.

At precisely eight o'clock the door bell rang, and Cara, who had just cleared away the remains of her meagre meal and was on the point of doing the washing-up, frowned perplexedly at the sudden summons that rang through the stillness of the villa. As she went to answer the door, her first thought was of her uncle. Perhaps he had decided to drop in on her, yet she knew it wasn't Uncle Theobald —he would do no such thing, not without notifying her first, and her chin stuck out a little further on her second guess. If it was Julia Besson, she wasn't going to find Cara as mute as she had been on other occasions—in fact, she was in for a battle royal if she did but know it!

On opening the door, her expression, that had held a certain determination together with a positive glint in her eye, underwent a rapid change when she saw who her visitor was. 'Oh, I wanted to see you,' she said on a note of pure relief, and stood aside for Pierre to enter the villa.

'And I wanted to see you,' was his grim answer as she followed his stiff back into the small lounge, and her relief changed to swift apprehension as she noted the way he had turned to face her after they had entered the room and now stood looking at her with narrowed eyes. 'Is it true?' he asked harshly. 'Are you the girl I caught trespassing on our property that day?'

Cara swallowed and nodded miserably.

'Then why the hell didn't you tell me who you were when you came to my office that day?' he demanded furiously.

Cara's hands twisted together. What could she say? She ought to have said something, she knew, but if she spoke the truth and said she hadn't wanted to embarrass him—or herself, come to that—or that she hadn't been given much chance of bringing such a subject up, surely he would understand? 'I didn't want to embarrass you,' she answered in a low voice.

'Thank you!' was his biting reply. 'And how do you think I feel now?' he queried in a soft dangerous voice that made Cara quake inwardly.

If it was anything like Cara felt, then it was pretty bad. 'Does Paula know?' she asked, before she gave herself time for thought.

'Miss Ericson unfortunately does know,' he replied coldly, and Cara felt as if she had been slapped in the face with a wet towel. It had been 'Paula' to her before—now it was 'Miss Ericson'. The 'old friend of the family' bit was obviously not strong enough to withstand the recent revelations!

'Someone made it their business to see that she was informed,' he said grimly, then gave her a swift calculating look. 'Any idea who that might be?' he shot out at her.

Cara knew very well that it could only be Julia's doing, and if he had stopped to think he would have reached that conclusion, too, but it wasn't for her to say. Truthfully, she couldn't be certain that it was Julia who had passed the news on to Paula, but there just wasn't anybody else interested enough to make that kind of mischief. 'I'm afraid not,' she answered steadily.

His eyebrows rose sceptically. 'Haven't you?' he queried. 'Well, I've a few ideas of my own on that, and I'm about to put them to the test!' he added grimly, and strode over to one of the easy chairs by the fireside and pointed to the matching one opposite it. 'Sit down,' he commanded harshly. 'I've a feeling we're in for a long session.'

As soon as Cara had seated herself, he sat down too, and settled himself comfortably into the deep cushioned chair, giving Cara the impression that if it took all night he was determined to get to the bottom of things. 'Now,' he said firmly, 'I'd like to hear the reason for your earlier reticence on this matter.'

Cara met his gaze steadily, then dragged her eyes away from his compelling ones and studied the tip of her shoes. 'I've already told you,' she replied in a low voice. 'I saw no reason to mention the incident.'

He studied her set features for a long moment, then said softly, 'What a pity; and I thought you were an intelligent person.'

'I like to think I'm still intelligent,' Cara retorted smartly, stung by the sarcasm in his voice.

'Then stop playing cat and mouse with me!' he bit back sharply. 'And grant me a little intelligence, too! You must have known you were putting me in a damned embarrassing position when you accepted the lease of the villa. You knew the past history of the place—yet you said nothing when a few words would have settled the matter—you knew I hadn't recognised you.' He stared at her with narrowed eyes, 'Perhaps it was pique that made you act as you did, but even after I had outlined my feelings on the past history of this place—you still said nothing.' He nodded grimly at Cara's swift flush in acknowledgement of this accusation. 'And all the time you sat there looking as if butter wouldn't melt in your mouth, although you must have realised you were sitting on a powder keg that was bound to be ignited some time in the future!'

Cara blinked in indignation at this strong and entirely uncalled-for observation on his part. 'That's not fair!' she retorted quickly. 'How was I to know that such a stupid incident would have caused such trouble? I would never have come back if I'd known this would happen.' She gave him a withering look. 'I'm surprised at you,' she remarked as her indignant eyes met his cold ones. 'I was so sure you wouldn't attach any importance to it. I'd forgotten it myself,' she added, then remembered the London restaurant episode and amended slowly as if talking to herself, 'At least. I had until ...' She stopped suddenly as she realised that it would be better if that part was left out.

'Until?' Pierre prompted her, but Cara was not to be drawn any further and closed her soft lips firmly as her gaze went back to her shoes again.

'Very well,' said Pierre, as if accepting her decision not to elaborate any further. 'Now I'll give my views on the matter, although I feel sure that there are quite a number of things you haven't been strictly honest about,' and he held up a lean hand to stem Cara's swift denial on this. 'Of course I didn't attach any importance to the incident you are referring to. I'm not that easily intimidated. I wasn't then, and I'm not now. It's the implication behind the event that worries me. Look at it from my point of view. I come across a girl trespassing on our property—a girl who had obviously run away from her village and by the look of the make-do shelter I found, had intended to stay for several days. I had no hesitation whatsoever in taking you back to where I thought you belonged.' He stared at Cara before adding on a vexatious note, 'Once again, a few words from you would have clarified the position. I was convinced I was dealing with a girl from the village—one does not expect to come across a young European girl living as a native in the tropical forest.'

He was silent for a few seconds as he recalled what happened that day, then shrugged. 'As for what took place when we arrived at the village ...'

here his intense blue eyes met Cara's wary brown ones.

'I can explain that,' she interjected swiftly, wanting to end this embarrassing interlude for both of them.

'I have given the matter a great deal of thought since then,' he carried on, totally ignoring Cara's intervention. 'And I could only come up with one reasonable explanation.' He paused a moment and gave her a long considering look, and there was something about that look that made her feel completely naked and she shrank from his cold appraisal. 'My apologies,' he said dryly, and this made things worse for her as she sensed what he was about to say. 'I could only deduce that you were in the habit of carrying out such escapades—a little promiscuous, perhaps, and that I just happened to be the unlucky one.'

By now Cara's cheeks were burning like a beacon in the night, and she jumped up out of her chair with a stiff propelling motion. His meaning was extremely lucid and she had no intention of allowing him further scope on this distasteful subject. 'If anyone was unlucky, it was me!' she flashed back at him. 'Do you know why I'd run away? I'll tell you why—I had just lost my father and had been told that I must leave the island and go back to England. I was given no time to get used to the idea. They were going to put me on a plane back within hours of the decision being made.'

She took a deep breath to enable her to make her point without breaking down and screaming at him. She felt let down, and all he past misery welled up, making her want to hit out at the man who was the cause of it all. If he had left well alone that day, she would have eventually returned to the village of her own volition, instead of being bullied into returning with him. All the resentment she had felt towards the man who had forced her to return now came back in full spate, and she not only resented him, she hated him for letting her down when she had been so sure that she could count on his good sense to put everything into its proper perspective.

At this thought she wanted to laugh hysterically; he was worse than Julia! She at least had a good reason for acting as she had, for it was sheer plain jealousy that had goaded her on, but what was his reason? As another thought came, her anger evaporated as quickly as it had arisen. Wasn't Paula a good enough reason? Had he lost Paula through her thoughtlessness? She looked across at him sitting watching her with that calm assured look that gave no hint of his feelings.

'I can also tell you why Tu-Tu took it upon himself to marry us,' she said quietly, not failing to note the quick haughty flash in his eyes as she said this. 'Polynesian fashion, remember,' she added on a sardonic note, 'and as such it formed no binding commitment on either of us. It was his way of providing for my future. He was a good friend of my father's, too.' She sighed, then continued, 'I also think he was well aware of the strict code of propriety practised by the Europeans, and I suspect that he felt that my father would have wanted such a ceremony carried out. What he failed to take into consideration was the fact that I was only sixteen and in European eyes was still a child and that there was no need for such a ceremony.' She ended the last sentence wearily; there was not much else she could add. Her anger gone, she felt only sadness for the past, and for what might have been her future had things been different.

Pierre said nothing for a few moments, but then as if thinking aloud he said, 'On the face of things, it all sounds very commendable, but unfortunately the episode has proved a powerful weapon for a person bent on mischiefmaking, and that could,' he reminded her sharply, 'have been nipped in the bud long before any damage was done.'

The damage, Cara presumed tiredly, being his break-up with Paula, and she had to accept a certain amount of responsibility for this. 'It was bound to come out sooner or later,' she answered slowly, 'and it could have been treated as a joke,' she added sadly. 'That would have put paid to any mischief-making.'

He studied her silently before he answered, as if trying to detect any sign of duplicity in her expression. 'I was not given a great deal of say in the matter, was I?' he reminded her grimly. 'There are other facts that seem to have escaped your attention, too. I have since learned that you were missing for three days before I came across you. I'm certain that that particular fact did not escape the old chief's reasoning in spite of what you thought was the motive behind his action. It won't escape others' reasoning either. There's only your word and mine that I didn't come across you earlier, and I don't have to spell out what interpretation might be put on that supposition, do I?'

Cara's eyes widened as she digested his words,

and even though she had discussed this aspect with Cathy, she still felt a sense of shock hearing it from him. 'Add to that interesting little snippet,' he went on grimly, 'the fact that I had you installed in this villa, and the grapevine will be working overtime. No, Miss Vernon, I am unable to view the matter as a joke, or if it is, it is a very distasteful one.'

'I entirely agree,' said Cara, finding it hard to keep her temper; he was only looking at things from his point of view. 'I had as good a reason as you had for not wanting the past brought up. That was why I said nothing,' she flashed back at him.

'At first, yes,' he agreed harshly, 'but something happened to make you change your mind, didn't it? I can't think of anyone else who would have enough interest in the affair to make that disclosure, can you?' he bit out at her.

Cara could, but there was no point in saying so, as he wouldn't believe her. It was Julia who had really put the cat among the pigeons. As for telling Paula about the past, Pierre must have forgotten her parting words at the airport. 'I didn't have to tell her,' she said witheringly. 'She knew about that before she came here.'

Pierre stared at her, and if his expression had been grim before. it was even grimmer now. 'And how do you happen to know that?' he asked silkily.

Cara started; now what had she done? It was too late to say that she presumed she must have known, he was a little too astute to swallow that. Her small chin came up in a gesture of defiance; he might as well know the truth. she told herself. 'I overheard something she said to you before you boarded the plane coming over here,' she told him. 'In fact, you collided into me as you turned to listen to what she was saying,' she added for good measure. Not that he would remember that, he had been too engrossed with Paula to notice her, she thought.

'For someone who had apparently forgotten the past, you seem to have taken an exceptional interest in me,' he said quietly, yet there was an element of distaste in his voice that made Cara feel the lowest of the low.

'It wasn't intentional,' she said firmly. 'I couldn't help overhearing what she said.'

'The interesting thing is that you had instantly recognised me,' he said musingly. 'Oh, I grant you that six years is not all that long ago, but I would swear that you took not the slightest notice of me that day. You were too busy sulking, if that is the right word. To you, I was a stranger who just happened to come across you and spoilt whatever machinations you had had in mind. You barely afforded me a glance, not even while the old chief was chanting his spell over us.'

Cara looked away from his speculating eyes and studied the carpet at her feet. Now was the time to tell him about the restaurant, and how she had happened to overhear a certain conversation between him and a few of his friends. Just what he would make of that she hated to think! He had already hinted that he didn't think much of someone who went around listening to others' private conversation. To report another such incident to him was out of the question—not even if her job depended upon it!

'And I wonder why you chose to come to me for a reference,' he added blandly. 'I would have thought I was the last person you would have applied to, considering how anxious you were not to bring up the past.'

Cara blinked in confusion; she wouldn't have gone to him if she had known who he was! Again she decided honesty was the best policy. 'I didn't know who you were then,' she said. 'I only knew your father had been my father's patron and I couldn't think of anyone else. I told you 'this at the time,' she added simply.

His closed expression told her that he didn't believe her. 'I'm afraid I find your explanation just a little too pat for comfort,' he said gratingly. 'Perhaps you feel unable to show your hand at this precise moment, although I have my own ideas on this. One thing I can tell you, and that is that you can forget whatever plans you had in mind for future appliance, where I'm concerned, anyway.'

Cara gave a gasp of outraged astonishment. She was sick of his veiled innuendoes. 'And just what do you think my plans, as you put it, are?' she demanded furiously. 'You might as well tell me. I prefer to have things straight.'

Pierre studied her out of narrowed eyes before he said quietly, 'Very well. I think you knew perfectly well that the day would come when the whole island would be aware of what happened six years ago. You couldn't have been so naïve as not to realise that. I believe that it must have been an added stroke of luck when I offered you this villa. It meant you were halfway there, didn't it?' he said meaningly. 'Do I have to go on?' he queried haughtily.

Cara stared at him, the amber flecks in her wide eyes now turned to pure gold that sparkled as her fury rose. 'Yes, please,' she said in a low tight voice.

Pierre gave her a disdainful look and Cara's hand itched to slap the expression off his haughty face. He then gave an expressive shrug as if to say that he didn't think further explanation was necessary. 'Perhaps you thought I might offer you marriage, on a more permanent basis, that is,' he said harshly. 'It would also explain why you took the trouble to put Miss Ericson into the picture.'

'It appears that great minds do think alike,' Cara said bitterly, remembering what Julia had said about her hoping for a civil wedding.

'I beg your pardon?' Pierre broke into her musings. 'Would you care to be more explicit?' His voice was low and very intimidating, but Cara was beyond intimidation.

'Offer me marriage?' she exclaimed in a voice that trembled with fury. 'Just you try, Monsieur Morelon! Oh, how I wish you would! Just to give me the pleasure of turning you down! As for being naïve—well, I have to admit to that. I really thought I could come back to the island as if nothing had happened—and it hadn't, no matter how much importance small-minded people tried to attach to the past. As for your suggestive surmise as to what I'd been up to in the bush, well, I won't even bother to answer that. I've told you why I was there. I love this island and look upon it as my home, and that,' she ended furiously, 'is the only reason why I returned. Now, is there anything else you wish to discuss? I've told you the truth, and if you don't believe me, then there's nothing I can do about it.' She looked pointedly at the clock, 'I have to go out soon,' she added, although she had no such plans but felt she had had enough of this insufferable man's company for one evening.

'Then you'll just have to keep him waiting, won't you?' he said harshly. 'You're going nowhere until we've sorted this little lot out. You started it, and I'm going to see that you're in at the finish.'

'St-started it!' exclaimed Cara furiously. 'How did I start anything?' she demanded.

'By a word here and there,' he said softly. 'I think that was going to be the way of it. This is a small island, Miss Vernon, although I hardly need to point that fact out to you, I'm sure you took that into account long ago. So it might be worth your while to listen to a proposition I'm going to put to you. You either play things my way, or accept the consequences.'

CHAPTER NINE

CARA'S wide eyes echoed her thoughts. He had called it a proposition, but had made it sound more like an ultimatum, and she felt an apprehensive shiver run through her very being. Whatever Pierre had in mind, she wasn't going to like—of that she was certain.

'Cheer up,' he said casually. 'If your expression is anything to go by, then you're very apprehensive. Things went sadly wrong, didn't they? But all is not lost yet. If you are sincere in your wish to stay on Totorua then you'll co-operate with me. I can't promise you a rosy financial future, but at least you'll have a job and a roof over your head.'

'And if I don't?' Cara challenged with a glint in her eye.

'You'll find the island's not big enough for the two of us, and I have no intention of leaving,' he answered curtly. 'Well?' he demanded harshly.

Cara looked away from him. Either she obeyed him or she left the island. It was as simple as that. 'It seems I haven't much choice,' she said bitterly, wondering whether it was going to be worth it.

Pierre gave an abrupt nod at this capitulation of hers, obviously satisfied with her reply. 'Now that's settled, I'll outline the position for you. Thanks to your interference, I find myself in an exceedingly unenviable position, since someone took it upon themselves to congratulate Miss Ericson on her engagement to me.'

Cara swallowed. She could almost imagine the scene—Julia seizing the chance of a private word with Paula and dropping a few delicate hints into her shell-like ear.

Taking due note of Cara's reaction to this piece of news, he nodded grimly. 'And that same someone,' he went on harshly, 'also took the trouble to bring up another side issue. I'm sure I can leave the actual phrasing to your imagination. Suffice it to say that Miss Ericson was left with the impression that I required extricating from what she termed as "an unfortunate attachment in my youth", and happily assured me that she had no objection whatsoever to my ingenious plan of using her as a cover.'

He gave Cara a hard stare and said savagely, 'As I at no time contemplated marrying Miss Ericson, I have no intention of placing myself under any such obligation from her. When it comes to ingenuity, I never fail to be amazed at the tactics employed by the feminine species of the race to obtain what they want,' he added bitterly. 'Of all the contracts Paula's been offered in the past, the marriage contract happens to be the one she won't turn down.'

Cara felt awful. Paula was beginning to sound very much like another Julia. 'I'm sorry ...' she began hesitantly.

'Hear me out,' he commanded haughtily before she could say any more. 'I think you will agree with me that the situation calls for drastic measures.' He glared at her. 'On your own admission, you were the only one who knew that Miss Ericson and I were well acquainted, and as this was her first visit to Totorua, it didn't take a lot of brain power to work out where that information came from. You rather miscalculated there, I'm afraid. You knew of course that Miss Ericson was a famous concert pianist—I doubt if that fact escaped your notice. Perhaps that is why you took the trouble to ensure that she was warned off what you considered your territory, you were probably thinking along the lines that she would shy from any situation that would bring bad publicity.' His lips thinned. 'But it all backfired, didn't it? Except for one small detail.' His eyes met Cara's incredulous ones. 'Your plan to involve me in a fictitious affair is about to become a reality, as far as Miss Ericson and the rest of the island are concerned, that is. I have already outlined my feelings on this to Miss Ericson, categorically stating that I am perfectly content with matters as they stand, and am quite definitely not in need of any such protection as she was proposing. I also,' he added meaningly, 'conveyed in no uncertain terms the fact that I found my little island bride's charms much too strong to resist.'

Cara's cheeks flamed a brilliant pink. 'How could you!' she exclaimed in a shocked voice.

'Very easily, as a matter of fact,' he continued smoothly, causing her blush to deepen even further, for there was a certain inflection in his voice that was not lost on her. 'You ought to have foreseen such an eventuality,' he observed lightly. 'This sort of situation is commonplace these days. You should be grateful,' he added casually. 'You could have been out of a job and on your way back to the U.K. by now.'

Cara wasn't too sure that she didn't prefer things that way; at least her reputation would be unsullied. 'I don't think ...' she began in a strangled voice.

'Then don't try,' he interrupted her harshly. 'You shouldn't start something you can't finish.' His eyes met hers inexorably. 'I said as far as Miss Ericson and the rest of the island are concerned, and I meant just that. I intend to spend a few night here a week—the gossipmongers will do the rest, enough anyway to satisfy any doubt Miss Ericson may or may not be harbouring. I shall be quite open about it, and I shall expect you to follow my lead. The affair will die a natural death upon the departure of Miss Ericson.'

A stunned Cara found herself wondering whether he meant to stay the night, and if he expected her to provide him with a meal. Thoughts like these were safe, others were not. She gave him a wary look under her long dark lashes. Did he really mean what he had said about only asking for lodgings for a few nights? It was only a front anyway, but when she remembered the way he had spoken earlier about her charms, she wasn't quite so sure. If he tried to take advantage of the situation he was in for a surprise, she told herself grimly. To think she had almost gone soft over him! He hadn't given one thought to her or the distasteful situation he was putting her in, he was too busy preserving himself from Paula's clutches—and to think she had tried so desperately to preserve their romance— or what she had thought was their romance!

'I agree to go along with you so far,' she said quietly, 'even though my reputation will be in shreds by the time this wretched business is over, but I don't suppose that fact will worry you. Have you thought of what my uncle might think when the news reaches him?' she demanded, suddenly having a vision of the extreme embarrassment it would cause him. 'And I must say,' she added, warming to her theme, 'is all this really necessary? It seems to me that I'm being put to all this inconvenience simply because you can't handle a woman. It might not be pleasant, but all you have to do is tell them you're not interested. Even Paula Ericson must have some pride!' she added pithily.

Pierre looked at her for a long moment before he said softly, 'So we have claws, have we? I'd advise you to keep them sheathed in future or you'll get more than you bargained for. Up until now I've acted the perfect gentleman, but there's no guarantee that I'll continue to do so. When I first walked in here I wanted to wring your neck for the mess you'd landed me in. Under the circumstances, I believe I've behaved very well. Any more remarks on my inability to handle a woman and you'll soon find that there's one woman that I can, and will handle—physically, if need be!' he ground out.

Cara tried to look indignant but wasn't sure if she succeeded, as her heart was pounding at an alarming rate at the thought of him manhandling her. Her steady eyes met his bright blue stare. 'There's no need to threaten me,' she said as calmly as she could. 'I've agreed to go along with you to allow you to create the necessary impression, but I sincerely hope for both our sakes that Miss Ericson's departure takes place in the very near future.'

Pierre gave her a wicked smile as he replied

lightly, 'Not too soon, I hope. I was looking forward to getting to know you. We've a lot in common, haven't we?'

Cara looked back at him with the gleam of temper in her eyes. He was having fun now at her expense, he had got the co-operation he had come for and could now relax. He had the looks and charm to enslave a woman, witness what had happened to Paula and Julia, but she was not going to join that entourage. His eyes were really twinkling now, almost as if he sensed her thoughts.

Women were weak where such men were concerned, she thought shrewdly, and he would know just how to play on their emotions. Without thinking she spoke her thoughts aloud, it was a sad failing that she really would have to do something about. she told herself afterwards. 'I'm glad I have no such weakness,' she declared fervently.

Pierre continued to study her; his eyes had now taken on a deeper blue, and she had an uncomfortable feeling he had correctly interpreted her line of thought. 'Haven't you?' he said softly after a long moment. 'Well, we'll see, won't we?'

Cara's hands clenched into small fists; she wished she could hit out at him, and only the distinct possibility of him making a retaliation stopped her, for she was not sure what form it would take. This time she was certain that he knew exactly what she wanted to do, as the look of amusement in his eyes plainly said, 'Coward!'

Just as suddenly as he had reverted from the annoyed to the amused mood, he resumed his initial authoritative approach as if he had spent enough time dallying with her. 'I shall not be presuming upon your hospitality this evening. Tomorrow, per-haps,' he said grandly. 'I have a key to the door.'

It was said simply, yet it made Cara feel exactly what the rest of the island would shortly be label-ling her, Pierre Morelon's woman! As if to stave off the inevitable she said swiftly, 'I might be out when you call. I do have a private life, you know.'

'You mean you had!' Pierre said meaningly, all previous amusement gone. 'I want your full co-operation on this, and no half measures. Parties or any evening entertainment are out for you from now on. You wouldn't want me seeking you out and acting the jealous lover, would you? Well, neither would I,' he added grimly. 'But make no mistake, I shall do just that if I have to. I have a lot at stake, remember? If there's any hopeful wooer of yours in the background, then shake him off. You stay put,' he said harshly. 'I know the ropes, you see,' he added bitterly. 'I've seen it all before.'

For a long time after he had left her, Cara re-mained where she was, staring at the frilled curtain-ing of the sitting-room windows. She didn't feel in any sense outraged, yet she ought to have done. She only knew a sense of sorrow for the man who had swept back into her life bringing such devastating events in his wake, for in his last telling words lay the reason for his extraordinary behaviour.

Outwardly he was a kindly, charming, and ex-tremely handsome man, but under that calm façade of his lay a bitterness towards the past. Cara had known that he disliked Julia, she had not been mistaken earlier in thinking that his dislike went beyond the normal reaction of not taking to someone, and she had sensed this at the time. Perhaps she was like her mother in looks, and this would certainly account for his feelings on the matter. It would also account for the fact that he was a bachelor, and meant to remain one. Paula hadn't stood a chance, and in a way Cara felt sorry for her, as she would have done for any woman who fell in love with him. Cara couldn't have explained how she knew all this about him, yet she did know.

Everything now fell into place; the way he had at first treated her harshly, then appeared amused at her calm acceptance of the situation. He did not think she was a blackmailer as he had hinted during the early part of their confrontation, for if he had thought so, he wouldn't have given her the time of day, and certainly would not have placed himself in jeopardy by making such a demand on her. He had known he could handle Cara, whereas Paula presented quite another problem.

Cara could now see why he had had to act as promptly as he had. Paula Ericson was a well-known personality and as such her life style would be of interest to her countless fans. She had only to mention the news to her agent and it would make headlines in musical circles. Before he knew what was going on Pierre would find himself being interviewed by one of the women's magazines eager to obtain a scoop on the news.

She moved away from the spot she had been standing on for so long and nodded her head slowly. Yes, that was what would happen. She could almost hear Paula's throaty, 'I'm so sorry, darling, but you know what the publicity hounds are like, one whiff of a secret and they move in.' And 'darling' wouldn't stand a chance, thought Cara shrewdly as she made her way to the room she would have to get ready for Pierre.

The same claustrophobic feeling overcame her as she gazed round at the peach fluffiness of the room, and she shook her head. He would not use this room, the very sight of it would fill him with repugnance— and that meant that he would have to use the room she had commandeered for her own use.

She sighed at the thought, she would have to move into this room. Going back into the small bedroom she emptied the drawers of the dressing table and took the articles of clothing into the main bedroom and placed them in the drawers of the ornate dressing table. She might as well be prepared for his visit as she would receive no previous warning.

At no time did it occur to Cara to be worried or fearful of his presence in the villa, in spite of those mocking blue eyes of his she knew now she would be perfectly safe with him, and she wasn't sure whether to be glad or sorry about this, for she was certain he would not abuse her hospitality, as he had phrased it.

While Cara got out fresh linen and made up the beds, it did occur to her that she ought not to be taking things quite so calmly, and she wondered if the events of the past few days had made her shock-proof! Here she was, calmly preparing a room for a man she scarcely knew, who was making use of her home in order to start a rumour flying round the island. At this point she corrected herself—the rumour was already rife—he was just fanning the flames by adding a touch of authenticity to it.

Cara sat down suddenly on the bed; had she inherited her father's knack of turning a dramatic situation into a comical farce? She must have done, she thought a little bewilderedly. By this time she ought to be dwelling on other things, such as how she was going to cope with the curious stares she was bound to receive, and the doubtful side-glances, not to mention a few leers from other men. Would she take all that as calmly as she was taking Pierre's decision to use her as a blind to forestall Paula's plans?

She had a vision of Cathy, and found herself giving a weak grin. If only she knew what she was missing! Perhaps one day she would tell her about it—but on this thought she sobered. It wasn't really funny, nothing was funny any more. Everything had a dreamlike quality about it, like this room, she thought, as she stared at the peach silk bedspread on the bed.

She ought, she thought sardonically, to have given him this room. If anything was calculated to bring the bizarre business to an expedient end as far as her involvement was concerned, this room would! One look and he would be busy making other arrangements—and Cara couldn't blame him!

She got up from the bed and went downstairs again, then wandered into the small patio at the back of the villa that overlooked the rockery, beyond which were the scented bushes of a white star-shaped flower that gave a luminous glow.

Even though it was now night, the rays of the huge southern moon lent enough light for her to still make out the villa boundary. There was but one consolation for her in all this upset, and that was that she would be able to stay on the island. Her job, too, had been saved, and surely the discomfort she would have to endure, if only for a short period in time, was worth the prize.

In her mind's eye she saw Pierre again, and the way he had sat watching her every reaction and wondered what he really thought of her. There had been so much she had not been able to explain; how can you explain coincidences like that? No wonder he was sceptical and held certain reservations on her motives, for although Cara had decided earlier that he did not see her as a blackmailer, she had also to concede to herself that whatever her motives had been, he was satisfied that he could handle them.

At least he did not hate her—although hate was a strong word. He did not hate Julia either, only for what she stood for, and for the self-centred way she had gone about reaching her goal, and as Pierre had once commented, she was very like her mother.

The strains of a Polynesian love song drifted towards her as she sat lost in her thoughts. It would have come from one of the pavement cafés now catering for the tourist season, and for a moment she listened to the soft seductive melody. Where was Pierre now? Was he wining and dining Paula in an effort to dissuade her from her crusade on his behalf? Not if that kind of music was being played anywhere in their vicinity, she thought dryly; if he had any sense he would organise a dinner party or some such entertainment, there was safety in numbers! Although, she mused, he had said something about a business engagement.

Her musings ended abruptly as a certain thought came to her and a bright flush stained her cheeks. What was she thinking of? What was it to her what he was doing? He could entertain all the island beauties for all it concerned her! She was even starting to think much as a mistress might think! Wondering where her man was when he wasn't with her.

Her man—the very thought made her jerk herself away from the patio and the soft persuasive beat of the music that was penetrating not only the air but an exposed part of her heart, and shut herself inside the villa, but there was no getting away from the thought. It taunted her as she tried to apply her mind to more mundane things such as whether she had enough orange juice to cater for two at breakfast should he appear on Sunday night.

After a while she gave up the struggle and gave full rein to her thoughts. Certain things had to be faced, and it came as a surprise to her that she was just as vulnerable as any other woman was when it came to a certain charming man. A man, she reminded herself sharply, who had no aversion to dallying with an attractive woman, but had no intention of committing himself at the altar.

Considering what must have been a sad childhood for him, Cara could well understand his motivation, and in a way it helped her to play her part—just as long as she could keep herself from becoming emotionally involved. She felt she owed him that much at least, and not only her, for her father's sake too, since aside from all other issues, her family was in debt to the Morelon family, and this was one way she could repay that debt. To give Pierre credit, he had mentioned no such obligation, though Cara was well aware of it.

The following day Cara made herself keep busy; she wrote several letters, one to Ermyntrude, in which she reported her work scene, and any other item that might be of interest to her, not forgetting to report on her Uncle Theobald and how he had settled down in his new environment. Ermyntrude, Cara suspected, had a soft spot for her uncle, mainly because there was a likeness between the brothers, and even though the marriage with Cara's father had not worked out, Ermyntrude remained loyal in her affections. This predilection for Uncle Theobald was unfortunately not reciprocated by him, for Cara clearly remembered a visit of his to Devon to meet his brother's new wife shortly after they were married. After spending what must have been a harassing ten minutes with Ermyntrude while waiting for his brother to return from visiting a patient, Cara had met him in the hall on his hurried way out to greet his brother whose car was just pulling up in the drive outside the house and had heard his muttered, 'The woman's mad!' as he went to meet his brother, in all probability to commiserate with him!

A small smile played round Cara's soft lips as she recalled the scene. Ermyntrude had been nervous, and a nervous Ermyntrude's conversation would be twice as difficult to follow as her normal dizzy contribution was!

Cara then wrote to Cathy, a much longer letter this time since she had received a nice chatty one from her that gave her all the news at her end. It appeared that she had settled down well at her new job and had no complaints, apart from the fact that there were times when she suspected that the staff were being indoctrinated into accepting the same culinary fare as the inmates, and when you considered that they were all on a strict calorie diet it was easy for Cara to imagine Cathy's indignation. A little on the plump side, Cathy had always had to watch her weight, but there was a limit, and as she had told Cara, 'There's a lot of me to keep going. It's a good job I hit it off with the cook!'

Cara answered the letter much in the same vein and gave her a run-down on a typical working day for her, taking care not to mention that her working conditions were not what one might call ideal owing to one member of staff. To bring that up would mean mentioning a few other things and it was a little too complicated for Cara to go into, although Cathy would never forgive her for keeping her in the dark, if and when she ever heard the ins and outs of the business.

It was when Cara came to the scrawled postscript at the bottom of Cathy's letter that said, 'By the way, have you met you know who?' that she had problems. In the end, Cara added a nondescript message that she had 'seen him around' and left it at that, hoping for Cathy's forgiveness at some future date.

By lunch time there was a coolness in the air that suggested rain, and Cara welcomed the thought. Rainfall in that part of the world came as a welcome diversion from the continually sunny weather, for the fall would be invigorating and not like the damp overcast showers that were all too often experienced at home, and had a nasty habit of turning into a deluge at the very mention of a vicarage fête!

An hour later the shower had come and gone, leaving the greenery brighter and the perfumed air even more pungent than before. Cara settled herself in the patio and tried to wish the hours away until the evening. As time went by she was getting increasingly nervous, and hated herself for her cowardice. At this rate, she told herself scathingly, she would do a good imitation of Ermyntrude when, and if, Pierre put in an appearance.

At two o'clock she received a phone call, and nearly fainted with relief when she heard Maaua's voice on the other end of the line asking her if she would like to join a beach party, and she consented gladly. The invitation couldn't have come at a better time, she told herself happily. Maaua must have second sight to have come to her rescue so propitiously.

Of course she didn't know how long the beach party would last. Some of them could go on for hours, she knew; as long as the food was there one just lazed about and enjoyed oneself. Ought she to provide something in that line? she wondered, then decided Maaua would have said if she was expected to bring something, but she hadn't.

All these thoughts went through her mind as she searched out her swimsuit, changed into it and slipped a cotton blouse and skirt over it to wear down to the harbour where she was meeting Maaua. It was safer thinking about these things than concentrating on others, such as her absence when Pierre arrived, and a sneaking feeling that she was letting him down.

He had a key, hadn't he? she told herself in an attempt to stifle her conscience, and who was to know that she was not in the villa? She had no neighbours to note her movements, so could come and go without observation, particularly if she took the same route as she took to go to work, through the covered archway. Not that Pierre would use the same exit or entrance, he would come via the boulevard, leaving his car in the space allotted for trading vans to pull off the road when delivering goods to the busy town centre. The gleaming Mercedes would be instantly recognised by the locals, and well he knew it, she thought with a gulp. That was what he had meant by the news being passed on by the gossipmongers, and the fact that it was there all night . . . She practically raced out of the villa on this thought, and almost forgot to collect a towel, then remembering it at the last moment snatched one up and made for the harbour.

CHAPTER TEN

ALTHOUGH the rain had cooled the air, the pavement stones felt warm under Cara's sandalled feet as she made her way towards the harbour, but she was only vaguely aware of this. Reaction had now set in and she was already regretting her action. After all that calmness she had shown earlier, both in Pierre's presence and in her own later musings, why had she suddenly panicked?

Her lovely eyes were clouded with uncertainty as she stared ahead of her, seeing, yet not seeing, the gay panorama going on around her, the family groups, each member carrying some contribution to a picnic on the beach. There were the tourists too, intent on making the most of their short stay on the island, their cameras clicking away happily at anything and everything.

It was this uncertainty that made her keep going; she needed something to do, and above all she needed company. Nearing the harbour she passed a small group of young servicemen and answered their shouted query as to where the best beaches were to be found, and walked on, knowing that they had hoped she would suggest that they followed her, as the towel slung casually over her arm gave ample proof of her destination. She felt mean as she quickened her steps in case any such request should be put to her, but she had no intention of getting lassoed into their party. They would not be short of feminine company for long, Cara knew, for someone would be bound to take pity on them and invite them to join one of the numerous beach parties going on around them.

One never need be lonely here, she mused as her eye caught Maaua's waving hand in the distance. Hospitality was a natural gift among these people of the islands. Outgoing themselves, they could not understand the Westerner's natural inbuilt reserve. The wonderful gift they had of accepting strangers into the family circle was something not even the well-meaning but totally misguided missionaries of the past had failed to eradicate.

'I'm so glad you could come,' Maaua said happily, as she took Cara's arm and led her towards three girls guarding a picnic hamper. 'It's a "ladies only" do,' she grinned. 'We've all got boy-friends who are tied up this afternoon, so we thought we would all get together. That way we can alibi each other,' she added with a chuckle.

Cara smiled back at her; it was an arrangement that suited her perfectly, she had as much cause to watch her step as apparently Maaua and the girls had.

After the introductions had taken place, Cara learnt that the girls, like Maaua, were nurses, and worked at the hospital. The chatter was gay as they made their way past the marina where craft of all descriptions bobbed alongside one another and the bright painted colours of the luxury yachts were reflected in the clear sparkling water around them.

Cara took a deep breath of sheer contentment; the very atmosphere was one of peace yet bustle—and it would always be so—not just in the summer

months as in England, where in winter the coast
lay sleeping in a shroud of mist and those brave
enough to risk a walk on the promenade were lashed
at by the high waves driven inshore by the fury of
the prevailing winds. This, she thought, as her eyes
dwelt on the scene before them as they neared the
beach of silver sand that stretched for miles along
that part of the coast, broken only by the tall king
palm trees that gave the impression of standing
sentinel against the intrusion of the tropical forest
behind them, this was for ever.

Everything else dwindled into nothingness as her
eyes caressed the shoreline, where the gentle waves
lapped against the gleaming sand in a soothing,
loving action. Her look moved on to the skyline
where tiny clouds hovered above the brilliant blue,
looking like puffs of cotton wool. She drew in a
breath of wonder, for she felt herself soaring as
though she had wings above the warm sand she
stood on, as if she had become one with the island,
and at that moment she knew with utter certainty
that the island was welcoming her back in its own
special way, and she wanted to cry tears of pure
joy for the magic of the moment.

A call from Maaua asking her if she thought this
was an ideal place for them to settle for their picnic
broke Cara's spell, and she gave her attention to the
matter.

The spot chosen afforded them room to spread
out without infringing themselves on other groups
around them, and the girls settled down to sunbathe
before going for a swim.

As Cara lay back on her towel and felt the warm
rays of the sun seeping through her recumbent body,

she listened idly to the girls making lighthearted conversation on various happenings in the wards during the week. It was part of a world that she knew and understood, and she felt utterly relaxed and content. The earlier prick of conscience that she had felt had evaporated upon learning that each girl had a heavy date that evening with the said boyfriends, and that the party would be breaking up around six o'clock. There would, Cara thought happily, be plenty of time for her to get back to the villa if Pierre should call.

Later, she bathed with the girls in the clear translucent water, and let the heat of the sun complete the drying process afterwards, giving her long blue-black hair a vigorous rub with the towel to remove most of the wetness.

The contents of the hamper were then explored, and the chicken leg Cara sat chewing a few minutes later couldn't have tasted better if it had been served on a silver platter. The soft sweet rolls filled with the hearts of young lettuces, eaten with the chicken, added to the repast. This was followed by a large slice of a heavily fruited cake that put Cara in mind of a Christmas cake, only without the embellishment of marzipan and icing, but just as enjoyable. There was also fruit to round off the sumptuous feast. Large succulent oranges the size of grapefruit, and rosy crisp apples, and lastly coffee, served out of a large flask. As simple as the meal was, it was the most enjoyable one Cara had ever had.

The hours flew by and soon the girls were repacking the hamper. Cara, helping to stack the crockery away, saw with delightful surprise that her tan had returned, for her bare arms compared favourably with the other girls' honey-coloured arms, and she no longer looked out of place amongst the rest of the sun-worshippers sprawled out around them.

Before they separated, Maaua suggested that they do the same again the next time they found themselves deserted, and they were all in accord with this suggestion, but next time Cara asked to be allowed to provide the food as she hadn't contributed anything this time. The girls then went their separate ways to prepare for the evening's entertainment.

Cara rather envied their obvious enthusiasm for the evening ahead of them, and wished she felt the same way, for she was beginning to dread an evening spent in Pierre's company. What, for goodness' sake, would they talk about all evening until it was time for them to retire? Cara quickly thrust this thought to the back of her mind; time enough for that embarrassment when it happened.

It was a few minutes past six when she let herself into the villa, and as the scent of cigar smoke assailed her senses she knew Pierre was there.

So soon, she thought bewilderedly, as she entered the sitting-room to find him sitting in a chair by the window with a sheaf of papers spread out on the floor beside him, one of which he was studying.

For a few moments she stood there waiting for his attention, and when he looked up at her there was something in his expression that made her feel like a little girl caught out in some misdemeanour, and she resented this. 'I didn't expect you so early,' she said, with a shade of defiance in her voice.

'Evidently not,' he replied dryly, then with slow

deliberation he studied her slight figure, her simple white sleeveless blouse that accentuated her golden tan, and the blue cotton flared skirt with its small waist and the slim brown legs, with feet encased in sandals. His gaze went back to her face again and rested on her blue-black hair now lying loose on her shoulders and he nodded to himself. 'You should have looked like that when you came to my office,' he said slowly, 'I might have recognised my child bride then,' he added amusedly.

Cara felt the colour flood into her cheeks at this extremely provocative remark. He wasn't being exactly helpful in keeping a low profile on the past, was he? 'I'm no longer a child,' she said coldly. 'I've grown up, or perhaps you haven't noticed? And I wish you wouldn't keep referring to that,' she added heatedly. 'It's a little late to joke about it now, isn't it, considering the mess we're in.'

A wicked smile spread across his lean tanned face showing white strong teeth that gleamed, and this further infuriated Cara. He was enjoying himself! She hadn't been wrong when she had suspected this before. His blue eyes were still twinkling when he answered soberly, 'Are we in a mess? I don't see that the situation is so obnoxious. At least, not to me, and yes, I had noticed,' he added, his eyes now taking on a darker hue as they lingered on her heart-shaped face. 'I have an odd feeling that ...' he left the rest of the sentence in mid-air, but Cara caught the drift of his thoughts and her heart gave a painful lurch. If he was playing with her, she would hate him for eternity. It was all too easy for him she thought bitterly, and wished she could ask him to leave. He was quite able to look after himself, cru-

sading Paula or no—or was that just an excuse?
Had the idea of taking up with her appealed to him?
She must present quite a change from his past
sophisticated lady friends, and her small jaw firmed
on the thought.

'I don't play those kind of games,' she said
abruptly, once more trapped into revealing her
thoughts, and a second later wished the floor would
open up and swallow her.

Pierre placed the documents he had been studying down on the floor beside the others, and got up
slowly and came over to where she was standing,
never taking his eyes off her for a moment, but Cara,
though trembling inside, held her ground and her
large brown eyes met his blue probing ones with a
steady clear gaze. 'Neither do I,' he said softly, 'and
you'd better believe it.'

There had been a firmness in his voice that frightened Cara and she looked away swiftly, not certain
what he was referring to; did he still think she had
some dark scheme in mind for future use? She
moved away from his side quickly. 'What time
would you like dinner?' she asked, trying desperately to sound offhand about it.

He chuckled at this abrupt change of conversation, and Cara thought bitterly that she was glad
that she amused him. 'We're eating out,' he said
casually, 'then we'll put in an appearance at my
home. Paula has invited a few guests in for the evening. We shall be expected to be there.'

Cara stared at him incredulously; having to put
up with the rumours and Pierre's presence in the
villa was one thing, but appearing by his side in

company was another! 'I'm sorry, but I don't think ...' she began faintly.

'Wear that white lacy thing,' he went on calmly, as if she hadn't spoken. 'I liked it.'

'White lacy thing.' Cara's befuddled thoughts were quite unable to grasp what he was talking about; how could he think of things like that—and how dare he tell her what to wear! she thought furiously when she realised that he was referring to the dress she had worn at the cocktail party.

The next moment she found herself swung gently round and given a little push towards the hall. 'I've ordered dinner for seven,' Pierre said firmly, 'so don't take too long over your toilet, will you?'

Apart from locking herself in her room and refusing to come out, there was simply nothing Cara could do about it!

The restaurant that Pierre took her to was quite near his home, and for a short while Cara thought they were actually going there until he turned off the main road and steered the big car down a narrow road off the highway that eventually brought them to a plush establishment nestled against the hills that overlooked the bay.

As it was just past sunset, lights were springing up from the various dwellings set on the hillside. Residences that could only be afforded by the wealthy, for their position commanded a breathtaking view of the sea and the surrounding countryside. The same went for the restaurant that they were now entering, Cara surmised, as her eye caught the gleaming silver on the snowy white cloths on the tables in the large ornate dining room they were shown into, and the waiters who glided noiselessly from table to table making themselves as unobtrusive as possible.

There was no music here to distract one from the culinary delights that undoubtedly awaited its clientele, but a hushed, almost reverent silence.

After handing Cara the large red and gold embossed menu, Pierre asked her if she had any dislikes, and Cara, who had not bothered to study the rather intimidating list of fare offered, shook her head since she was sure that whatever was ordered she would not enjoy, for she was dreading the social evening ahead of them.

Feeling a little like the condemned man about to partake his last meal, she listened as Pierre ordered the meal in his native language, and she thought how expressive and elegant the French language was. Some thought of it as the language of love, she mused, and on this thought she hastily applied her mind elsewhere; this was not the time to dwell on such a subject, considering the ordeal in front of her.

Her brooding eyes studied Pierre's dark head as he consulted the menu and gave the order. He was not in evening dress, although his dark blue striped business suit and immaculate white shirt with pin-striped tie had obviously passed muster in an establishment that would insist on evening wear for their patrons. In all probability, they had waived the rules for him as it was clear that he was not unknown to them as the head waiter had taken it upon himself to personally oversee proceedings.

When the food arrived Cara had to admit that the Entrecote Bordelaise was as delicious as it had looked as the waiter placed the chosen fare in front of them. To her surprise she was able to make a fair inroad into her portion of food, enough anyway to forestall any comment on her lack of appetite. Another fact also emerged during the course of the meal that rather surprised her, and this was their conversation; she was not sure whether it was Pierre's skilful handling, or whether they were completely in accord with one another. They spoke of England, and he told her of the time he had spent there managing his father's business affairs, and Cara spoke of the college she had attended and a little of Devon where she had spent most of her vacations with Ermyntrude.

By the time they had reached the chocolate George, a nest of meringues filled with chocolate cream, and laced with brandy, Cara was way past worrying about the next item on the evening's agenda, and as she sipped the delicious coffee later and tried a liqueur that Pierre recommended, she knew she was in love with him and would always be. It was a wonderful exhilarating feeling that made her feel slightly reckless, for she could not see that he would ever reciprocate that love, and rather suspected that he was making a point of being particularly charming to her in order to bend her to his will. He needed her full co-operation for the evening ahead of them, and was making sure that he received it.

It seemed the most natural thing in the world when he pulled her arm through his as they strolled towards the place where he had parked the car and Cara had no objection, not then anyway; tomorrow she might flay herself for her weakness, but tomorrow was another day.

When they arrived at his home, he escorted her

into the cool wide hallway with a courtesy that only her Uncle Theo could have emulated and she felt cherished, even though she did wonder if he was not overdoing things, and while loving every moment of such preferential treatment, she was not unmindful of the reason behind his actions.

The murmur of voices met them as they crossed the marbled floor towards the lounge, and the moment they entered the room Cara saw that Paula's guests were not what one might call social guests, for judging from the notebooks at the ready, Paula was in fact holding a press conference that she broke off as soon as she saw that Pierre had arrived.

'How long are you going to be here, Miss Ericson?' queried an earnest-looking, spectacled young girl.

Paula gave what Cara could only describe as a coy look towards Pierre and flung out a welcoming arm towards him. 'I think you'd better ask Monsieur Morelon that question,' she replied with a light laugh. 'Come over here, darling. As you see, I need your help.'

Cara felt herself caught round the waist and being propelled by Pierre's side to join Paula. 'We shall be very disappointed if you leave before our wedding, won't we, darling?' he asked Cara.

'Darling' was extremely grateful for the firm hold her 'fiancé' was then affording her, and at the extra pressure from his arm, she nodded dumbly in assent.

It seemed to Cara that time stood still from that moment, and she had a feeling that Paula felt exactly the same way, though she made a stout re-recovery with an acid sweet, 'Oh, I wouldn't miss that for the world!'

'What was the special announcement you promised to make?' demanded a young man with hair that was a trifle too long, and a badge pinned to his lapel that read, 'Music News'.

Paula flashed him a look of pure hate, and her flashing eyes rested for a second on Pierre before she answered haughtily, 'I have accepted a contract to go on a tour of the United States.'

'Didn't you say you'd had enough of touring and were thinking of settling down?' persisted the same young man, who had no idea he was dicing with death if Paula's look was correctly interpreted, or at best, loss of job in the very near future.

'There are times,' she answered smoothly, 'when everything gets on top of you, and you just want a break. I am resting now, but I am sure that I shall be more than ready to return to my career in a few weeks' time.'

If Cara had been wearing a hat she would have taken it off to Paula. Such was her admiration for the smooth way she had covered her tracks. The announcement she had promised the newsmen had nothing to do with a tour of the United States, of that Cara was certain, but was of a very different nature.

She turned her head to look at Pierre whose arm was still round her slim waist and met his questioning glance at her with a stab of apprehension in her heart, and without knowing why, she slipped out of his grasp and made for the door.

Paula was again immersed in answering various questions put to her, and there was no need for her presence. The crisis had been averted, and there was no call for any further play-acting on either her part or Pierre's.

When Cara got to the hall she realised that she had no transport and would have to wait for Pierre to take her back to the villa. She stood there for a moment or so, not wanting to go back to the lounge, but most of all not wanting to meet Pierre again. She knew she was being unreasonable and that he was waiting for her return, thinking that she had gone to the powder room.

'Going to desert me?' Pierre asked softly behind her, and her heart lurched as he gently pulled her round to face him.

Cara tried hard to meet his probing blue eyes, but failed utterly, and fixing her gaze on his tie she took refuge in an excuse. 'I'm not used to press conferences. They're a little overwhelming, aren't they? I mean, they don't give one much privacy, do they?'

'It's the price of fame,' he replied lightly, but his eyes continued to probe hers. 'I don't think we'll be bothered any more in that line, but if things get tough, I'll hold your hand if you'll hold mine,' he offered solemnly.

Cara's previous embarrassment vanished as she gave a choked chuckle, and allowed Pierre to take her back to the company.

Pierre's light offer to hold her hand should the going get tough was no idle promise, although Cara had thought it amusing but unnecessary. However, she was shortly proved wrong, for as soon as the press had left, Paula turned her attention to Cara.

Dressed in a black velvet gown that emphasised her curves, and her hair piled high in the classical style, she radiated beauty and assurance, but her eyes echoed her true feelings when she looked first at Cara, then at Pierre, who was replenishing their drinks. 'That was a foul thing to do,' she remonstrated in a low vibrant voice to Pierre.

He gave her a warning look before he handed her her drink. 'I have a distinct feeling that it might well have been me making that remark,' he replied airily, though there was a hint of steel in his voice that clearly told Paula to watch her step.

Paula was not in the mood to take any such advice, unspoken or otherwise. With her drink in her hand she paced up and down the long room in regal splendour as if it were impossible for her to stand still. 'You fool, Pierre!' she said vehemently, and seeing that Pierre had settled himself beside Cara on the divan, she flung her a furious look. 'I see no reason why she should still be around. She's served her purpose, hasn't she? Why don't you ring for a taxi for her?'

There was a tiny silence after this, and Cara, who entirely agreed with Paula's observations, actually made a move to get up, but Pierre's arm shot out and clamped her by his side.

'If anyone's de trop, my pet, it's you,' he said silkily, yet managing to inject a veiled amount of insolence in his voice.

Cara held her breath. And to think she had accused him of being weak and not being able to handle a woman! If he had spoken to her like that she would have crawled under the floorboards and taken up permanent residence there.

Not even the sophisticated Paula could withstand a remark like that and wisely took her cue. 'Thank you, Pierre,' she said haughtily. 'It's nice to know where one stands, isn't it?'

'I think you've always known that,' Pierre pointed

out, gently this time. 'I had hoped that we would still remain friends.'

Paula blinked hastily but refused to accept the peace offering. 'I hope you'll both be very happy!' she spat out, and on this doubtful sounding felicitation she swept out of the room.

Pierre took hold of one of Cara's trembling hands and turning the palm towards him kissed it slowly. 'Shall we be happy?' he asked her softly.

Cara attempted to pull her hand away, but he refused to relinquish it. She couldn't look at him, for there were tears in her eyes. She knew now what it felt like to love and hate someone at the same time. Her voice was as low as Paula's had been and just as vibrant, only emotion, not hate, tempered it. 'As Paula has just said, there's no need to go on with the play, is there?' she said bitterly.

'Who's playing?' he queried gently, and placed a finger under her small defiant chin, making her look at him. 'I'm not, and I wouldn't advise you to either.'

Cara's eyes met his in a long look; hers were wary, his were searching, and when she saw his gaze rest on her lips she pulled herself away from him. If he kissed her she would be lost, for she would not be able to prevent herself from responding in a way that would leave him in no doubt that she loved him, she was not experienced enough to be able to hide her feelings. 'Please take me home,' she said in a low impersonal voice.

She did not look at him—she couldn't, she was so afraid her misery would show in her eyes. Somehow she had to keep going until she got back to the villa, and then it would be over. She did not want his gratitude, at least, not in the way he had attempted to prove how grateful he was. A sincere 'thank you' was preferable to that.

His sigh was long and deep and spoke of disappointment, yet his voice was light as he said, 'Very well—I suppose I was asking a lot. There's time enough; come along, my obstinate one, your word is my command.'

Neither of them spoke on the way home, and Cara for one was very grateful for this intermission and used the breathing space to think up some light quip she could make before she said goodnight to him, then she remembered that she could thank him for the lovely meal. She must not be too polite about it, but try and act normally, for she had enjoyed that part of the evening. One thing did worry her, though; since the following day was a holiday it was quite possible that Pierre would attempt to make a date with her. He might feel obliged to do so, and Cara would have to turn him down without making a big thing about it, and try to keep things casual.

In the event, he made no mention of a meeting the next day, and Cara, womanlike, felt quite piqued about this. It was unreasonable of her, she knew, but she would have liked to have been given the option of saying yes or no to him.

With the same courtesy he had shown earlier, he walked to the door of the villa with her, but did not attempt to take her arm as he had done before, and this too rather hurt Cara, so when he took her key from her and inserted it into the lock, and gave her a light, 'Goodnight, Cara,' she was able to answer with just as much casualness, only remembering as she closed the door behind her that she had not thanked him for the meal.

It was only a little thing, yet it brought the tears to her eyes and unleashed the misery she had kept at bay for so long.

CHAPTER ELEVEN

By the time Cara sat down to her solitary breakfast the following morning, she had reached a more philosophical attitude towards life, having spent the previous night turning matters over in her mind. One part of her was regretting that she had refused Pierre's kiss, for he would have kissed her, of that she was certain, and wondering what his kiss would have felt like, longing to feel his firm lips crushing hers, but the other part of her, the sensible part, knew there would only be heartbreak in store for her if she had succumbed to temptation. This part of her was proud of her, proud because she had kept her head even though she had yearned to feel Pierre's strong arms around her.

In spite of her unhappiness Cara knew she had a lot to be thankful for; since Pierre could have forced the issue, he was astute enough to gauge her feelings, and she would have had no defence against him, but he had decided to abide by her decision. There could have been no other reason for the calm, almost polite way he had escorted her back to the villa and wished her goodnight without attempting to seek her company the following day. But why should he? she asked herself bitterly. He had got what he had wanted, and though Paula had guessed that he was only using Cara to thwart a master plan of hers to trap him into marriage, she was hardly likely to make another bid to capture his affections.

If anything good had come out of the evening for Cara, it was the fact that Pierre had announced that they were engaged, for as untruthful as the statement had been, it did release her from his earlier plan of using her as a cover and there was now no need for the nocturnal visits to be carried out.

He hadn't, she thought sadly, apologised for that, and he ought to have done. She put down the piece of toast she had been attempting to chew and pushed the plate away from her, her once healthy appetite completely deserting her.

Pouring herself some more coffee, she gazed down into the swirling golden liquid. He hadn't apologised for the same reason that he hadn't asked to see her again. He must have thought that he had got off lightly and wished to keep things that way. Well, he needn't worry; she had no intention of presuming upon their acquaintance, not even of accepting another cocktail invitation that she was sure she would be bound to receive if only to show her that he was grateful to her.

Her fingers clenched hard round the handle of her cup; if he so much as tried to thank her ... She took a deep breath—if he did, then she would say that she owed him that much at least. It was one way of paying her family's debt to the Morelon family. Only, her heart whispered, she wished it hadn't cost her so dear.

The telephone rang as she was clearing away the remains of her meagre breakfast, and as she went to answer it she was certain it was a wrong number, she had been getting quite a lot of those lately. On answering, she gave her number in a clear voice, advising whoever was calling of the number that they had rung, then waited for the usual 'Sorry wrong number.'

'Did you sleep well, *chérie*?' Pierre's lazy voice enquired.

Cara stood rooted to the spot and her nerveless fingers almost dropped the receiver, but she pulled herself together. 'Very well, thank you,' she lied.

'You did better than I, then,' he replied lightly, yet there was a teasing quality in his voice that made Cara want to put the phone down on him. 'I'll be over about six,' he went on casually. 'I meant to make it earlier, but an old business acquaintance has dropped in on me. Are you still there?' he queried, the amusement now plainly audible in his voice.

'Yes,' said Cara, 'but I don't know for how long,' and she meant just that!

'If you want to go and sunbathe for a few hours on the beach, I've no objection,' he told her authoritatively, 'but don't overdo it. Take a hat with you, sunstroke can be quite nasty.'

'Very well,' replied Cara carefully, thinking that she might as well humour him, since that was what was advised when dealing with distinctly odd people. He might have got a touch of the sun himself!

His parting words consolidated the sunstroke theory, if not something worse, for he murmured a few endearments in French to the effect that he would be counting the hours, and rang off leaving a decidedly worried Cara looking at her receiver.

Her knees were weak as she walked back to the sitting-room and sank slowly on to the nearest chair. The sunstroke theory was out, and she didn't at all care for the alternative explanation, but there was no other answer. Tears of frustration filled her eyes, and she resolutely blinked them back. This was not the time for weakness, she had some serious thinking to do.

Pierre had not accepted her decision to keep her distance from him, that much was plain, and what was worse, it very much looked as if he intended going through with the original plan, even though there was now no need for the follow-through. At least, she thought bitterly, not where Paula was concerned—as for Pierre—had he taken her refusal as a challenge? Had his pride been unable to accept that there was one woman who could stand firm against his devastating charm?

She wished it was as simple as that, but there was more to it. Deep in her heart she knew he was as attracted to her as she was to him; she had known it from the moment her eyes had smiled into his at the cocktail party, and she had fallen in love with him at that precise moment even though she had tried to ignore the fact.

She angrily brushed away a tear that had escaped and spilled over. What a time to think such thoughts! She was not the only woman he had been attracted to, and she would not be the last; it was not her fault that he had had a sad childhood, yet in a subtle way he was exacting payment from those unfortunate enough to come within scope of his magnetic attraction.

Poor Paula, she thought sadly, and she had thought her so lucky. Was she still at that impressive home of Pierre's? she wondered, hoping against hope that he would change his mind. At this point another thought entered her mind, and Pierre's call suddenly began to make sense. She was still there! She was sure of it; there had not been much time for her to arrange her departure—so that was it! She had tried to make a comeback and that call to Cara had been Pierre's answer!

Cara took a deep breath. So it did make sense after all, and there was no call for panic stations—or was there? Would he still come at six? She swallowed. If Paula was still at the villa, then he most certainly would come, but if she had departed ... She shook her head. He would come—there might be a lot of things she was not certain about, but not that!

She jumped out of her chair and started mechanically straightening the cushions on the divan that were perfectly straight before she started, but she needed something to do, anything that would take her mind off one tall and very charming man who had blue eyes that looked right through your very being, and who had only to hold his arms out to her and she would fling herself into them. She wouldn't care about the future, not then; it was afterwards that she would have to face up to that.

Feeling like a trapped animal, she stared around the room. She had to get out of this place, accepting the lease had been the start of everything, but where could she go? It was then that the hostel came to mind, and with it Maaua. Maaua would know how she could apply for residence.

The next moment she was searching for the hostel's number in the telephone book, and finding it her trembling fingers dialled the number. 'Please let her be in,' she whispered as she listened to the rings the other end as the connection was made.

When the call was answered she asked for Maaua and held her breath when the girl who had answered the phone said that she would see if she was there. A second later, Cara's pleas were answered and Maaua came on the line.

'Cara here, Maaua,' she said breathlessly. 'How do I get a room in the hostel?'

'You just apply,' answered Maaua, sounding a little puzzled. 'You work at the hospital, so you'll have no trouble. The room next to mine is empty at the moment. Do you want me to book it for you?' she volunteered helpfully.

Cara gave a sigh of utter relief that was not lost on the kindly Maaua. 'Oh, yes, please,' she breathed thankfully.

'Hold on, then,' Maaua said quickly, 'I'll just go to the office and see about it for you.'

Gratefully Cara hung on, glad that she had one friend that she could rely on.

'It's okay,' came Maaua's slightly out of breath reply, 'you can have the room. You just fill in a form when you arrive.'

'Can I come right away?' demanded Cara hopefully.

'Sure you can,' replied Maaua. 'I'll give you a hand with the luggage. Be right over.'

Cara replaced the receiver; bless Maaua, she must have been curious, yet she had not asked one question. Her step was light as she ran up the stairs and commenced packing. Her clothes were pushed in willy-nilly with no thought for neatness, just as long as they went in the cases. She couldn't wait to get out of the villa and all it represented.

True to her word, Maaua arrived just as Cara had finished packing, and together the two girls made their way to the hostel. There were three cases in all, Cara carrying the heaviest one and Maaua the two lighter ones.

Upon arrival at the hostel, Cara duly signed the register, and was taken up to her room by Maaua. It was large and very airy, and very impersonal, but that did not worry Cara. As far as she was concerned it was a palace, and she was sure she was going to be able to settle down there with no trouble at all and feel protected by the fact that she was one of many residents in the building, and would not be answering the telephone, particularly as she was on the first floor and the phone was in the hall on the ground floor.

With Maaua sitting on the bed gravely watching her as she unpacked, Cara knew the time had come to do some explaining. 'It seems,' she began lightly, 'that you were not the only one who remembered a certain happening on the day I left Totorua, and whoever else remembered it, passed the news on. I don't suppose they did it deliberately—not to make trouble, that is, but unfortunately a few people have made two and two add up to five.' She shrugged casually. 'I thought it might be better if I left the villa, less embarrassing, if you see what I mean.'

Maaua nodded, 'Could have been anyone,' she said musingly. 'There's several people from the village working at the hospital.' Her large brown eyes met Cara's. 'Sister Dufour's very good at ferreting out information,' she said slowly. 'I didn't say anything, Cara.'

Cara smiled at her, 'I know you didn't, Maaua,' she said gently. 'But I think I can see how the news got around now. In a way it was my own fault; I told her that I used to live on the island.' She sighed. 'Well, the damage is done now, and there's mischiefmaking about, and I'm not going to encourage that.'

'What does Monsieur Morelon say? Does he know you've left the villa?' Maaua asked.

Cara replied to the second half of the question, not wanting to discuss the first. 'No, he doesn't know as yet,' she replied tersely. 'It was my decision, but I'm sure he'll agree,' she added firmly. 'What are the mealtimes here, Maaua?' she asked quickly, wanting to change the subject.

Maaua told her, but was not so easily put off. 'I think you ought to have talked it over with him,' she said, reverting back to the earlier subject. 'He doesn't seem to be the kind of man who would take any notice of that sort of gossip,' she mused thoughtfully.

That, thought Cara wryly, was exactly what she had thought, but had since been proved wrong. There were, she had to admit to herself, a few more side issues to the whole business that could have been straightened out if she had only the sense to speak up at their first meeting. It was much too intricate to go into with Maaua, and the least said the soonest mended. Suffice to say that she had decided to leave the villa and leave it at that. 'Perhaps,' she said answering Maaua's observations, 'but I prefer things this way.'

To Cara's relief, Maaua had a date after lunch and would not be back until later that evening, and as fond as she was of Maaua, not to mention grateful, Cara was afraid that should they spend the rest of the day together, she would soon find herself telling her about Pierre's visit, and worse still, the ensuing events.

A short while after Maaua had left, Cara put a call through to her uncle, and when the club's receptionist could not locate him for her, she left her new telephone number for him to ring her later.

She spent the rest of the afternoon finding her way about the hostel, that although consisting of only two storeys, an island building regulation, still covered a wide area, and she was pleasantly surprised with the facilities provided. Everything had been catered for, from a laundry room to a room for study, the latter being very necessary as some of the girls were sharing accommodation and would invariably have to sit for exams at one time or another.

When it was six o'clock, Cara debated whether to stay in the hostel for her evening meal or go out to one of the roadside cafés, then she remembered that her uncle might ring her and that she ought to be there when he did. There was also the overriding thought that Pierre would be calling at the villa, and in all probability would go out looking for her when he found that she was not at home, and recalling his autocratic concession of not minding if she wished to spend a few hours on the beach, she thought he would probably head for the beach.

She swallowed. Yes, she was much safer where she was; he would not be in too good a mood when he realised that she was not going to play any more

charades with him, and that he would have to find
another leading lady.

Ten minutes after six there was a knock on her
door and a cheery girl told her that she had a telephone call. 'A man,' volunteered the girl. 'Asked
for Miss Vernon. I said we hadn't anybody of that
name here, but he said you were a new arrival—
so I asked in the office. My name's Kate, by the way,
my room's just off the hall so I usually get to answer
the phone,' she explained with a smile.

Cara smiled back at her. 'I'm Cara,' she said as she
followed the girl down the corridor. 'You won't get
many calls for me, but I did ask my uncle to ring
me.'

When she reached the hall where the telephone
was located, she searched about in her mind for a
plausible story to tell her uncle as to why she had
left the villa, and by the time she picked up the receiver an excuse had come to mind. She would say
that she was lonely and had decided to move in with
the other girls from the hospital. He would understand that, for he had said at one time that she might
find it a bit lonely on her own. 'Hello, Cara here,'
she said quickly.

'I hope you haven't unpacked,' came Pierre's
smooth voice on the other end of the line, 'because
you'd better start packing again. I'll be over to pick
you up in fifteen minutes' time. I need an occupant
for that villa,' he added harshly.

Cara gasped at his audacity. 'I'm sure you'll have
no trouble in finding a new tenant,' she answered
curtly. 'I'm staying here.'

'You'll damn well do what you're told,' he replied furiously. 'Fifteen minutes, I said. If you're

not ready then, I'll help you with the packing, understand?' The receiver was slammed down his end, leaving Cara staring at her silent one.

He couldn't—he wouldn't—— She swallowed. Oh, but he would—of this Cara was in no doubt! He had evidently decided he would rather deal with her than with Julia. If the villa was empty, Julia would make another bid for the lease and this time he would be hard put to it to refuse. For one mad moment Cara considered ringing her at the hospital, and if she wasn't there, finding out where she could be located and putting her into the picture. She could rely on Julia to do the rest, something on the lines of, 'I've moved into the hostel, if you're still interested in the villa, you should apply for the lease.'

She glanced at her watch. Five minutes of that fifteen minute deadline had passed and still she stood in an agony of indecision. Finally she made a dash back to her room and started packing. It wasn't that she was a coward so much as she had a good imagination and could see what would happen if she attempted to stand her ground.

Pierre was so well known that his visit to the hostel was bound to cause a few speculative remarks, and if he dragged her out as he had threatened to do, then the place would be agog with the news. At least, she told herself firmly, she would go of her own free will, for the moment anyway, but would not cancel her room. She might not get another one and the chances were that she would need a bolthole in the very near future!

As she carried her suitcases down to the entrance of the hostel, Cara found herself fervently hoping that her departure was not observed, and as it was a holiday her hopes were fulfilled, for there was not one onlooker to her furtive departure proceedings, and wishing to keep this state of affairs she moved her cases out of the hostel and a little way away from the entrance.

The crunch of wheels on the gravel drive of the hostel told her that Pierre had arrived, and she barely glanced at him as he relieved her of her luggage and put it in the Mercedes. She did not acknowledge his brief, 'Well done!' either, but silently followed him back to the car and got in the front passenger seat as indicated by him.

As they travelled the short distance back to the villa Cara kept her eyes straight ahead, well aware that her companion gave her several speculative side looks from time to time. He was extremely pleased with himself, that much she knew, and she wished she could flatten his ultra-ego. His attitude gave her food for thought, too, almost as if he had not expected her to toe the line, yet she was practically certain that the fact that she might not agree to return to the villa had not even been entertained by him. He was too used to getting his own way, so it had to be something else.

When they arrived at the villa, Pierre opened the door with a key he selected from his key ring, and the action gave the now wary Cara a tiny shock, for she still had her key in her pocket, and the action gave her a sense of outrage, even though he had told her that he had a key to the villa.

After placing her cases beside the stairs, Pierre gave an abrupt nod towards the sitting-room and Cara had no choice but to go ahead of him, but the storm signals were gathering in her eyes as she took the lone chair by the window, indicating her annoyance with his high-handed action. 'I'm not staying,' she said, as firmly as she was able, 'and apart from locking me in, there's nothing you can do about it!' she added challengingly.

'And I,' he said meeting her eyes warningly, 'do not intend to let my fiancée take up residence in a hostel—any hostel, we'll have that understood for a start. I want you where I can reach you at any time, and I certainly do not intend to have my telephone calls relayed by half a dozen young ladies, or messages passed on.'

Cara blinked at him, 'Not half a dozen,' she murmured bemusedly, 'only Kate,' then caught herself up. She must be as crazy as he was! 'We're not engaged,' she said swiftly. 'I have only been introduced as your fiancée to get you out of a mess.'

'In front of a dozen press men,' he reminded her cruelly, yet he was smiling.

'Then we'll give another press conference,' she retorted smartly, stung by his obvious amusement at the situation. 'This time we'll revoke it. We can have a public row if you like,' she offered sarcastically.

'We'll have a thundering row long before that if you don't stop baiting me,' he growled ominously. 'You should have spoken up then, it's too late now. If you've any second thoughts you can forget them.'

Cara stared at him dumbfounded, 'S-second thoughts!' she spluttered. 'I didn't have a chance, and you know it!'

He gave a complacent nod at this. 'What else did you expect? I wasn't going to risk actually asking you, not after you'd given your views on the matter earlier, so you can take it as read. I thought perhaps the seventh of next month,' he went on casually. 'That will give you time to work a month's notice. You won't want to leave them in the lurch, will you?'

Cara continued to stare at him, wanting to shake her head to clear the fog that had descended on her senses, then a wave of fury washed over her. Who was doing the baiting now? 'Not the seventh,' she ground out, 'not of next month or next year, or ...' she stopped in mid-sentence as she watched Pierre take a purposeful step towards her.

'I warned you once,' he said with a glint in his eye that frightened her.

She got up from her chair and took a step back, then found her retreat cut off by the window with Pierre still advancing. 'Don't you dare touch me, Pierre Morelon!' she cried, now really frightened. 'Can't we talk this over sensibly?' she pleaded.

Pierre took one last step towards her and pulled her into his arms, then looked down into her wide eyes and then at her soft full lips. With a gentleness she did not think him capable of, he kissed her lightly, his lips only touching hers for a brief second, and moving on to caress her closed eyelids. 'Give up, *chérie*,' he said softly. 'I knew from the moment you walked into my office that I was going to see a lot more of you. Call it fate, or what you will—we belong.'

His lips descended on hers again, but no longer gently; it was as if he had to prove to her that she was his and he would brook no denial. Whatever Cara had thought his kiss would be like, it surpassed her wildest dreams, and she was lost to all else but the fact that she loved him desperately.

When he did give her respite, he looked down at her flushed countenance and over-bright eyes from out of which shone the love that he had evoked, and with a groan he pulled her hard against his body, so close that she could feel his beating heart. 'A month's too long, *chérie*,' he said in a voice that told her how much he wanted her. 'Perhaps you ought to go back to that castle after all.'

'And have our messages relayed?' she teased him lightly.

He gave a grin and kissed her swiftly. 'Be it on your own head, then. I think perhaps I'd better throw a few more parties!' He looked down at her hand now resting on his arm and studied her slim fingers. 'What kind of ring would you like?' he asked.

Cara's eyes filled with tears of happiness as she whispered, 'An island ring of coral.'

His answer was to crush her to him once more. 'Whatever my lady desires,' he said huskily.

A short while later, she stirred in his arms and looked up into his strong face. 'Are you hungry?' she asked, thinking that he had probably missed his evening meal.

Pierre's eyes twinkled back at her. 'Very,' he said solemnly.

Cara blushed rosily. 'I didn't mean that,' she said primly, correctly interpreting his meaning. 'You know what I meant.'

He put his dark head against her cheek. 'Are you?' he countermanded, putting the ball into her court.

Cara sighed. 'Not really, but I do think we ought to move. I don't really want to go back to the castle, as you put it.'

With a gentle push Pierre tipped her off his knees and out of the chair they were sharing. 'We'll have dinner out, then,' he said grandly, adding a warning of, 'If you're not ready in ten minutes flat—we stay.'

Cara needed no second warning and picking up the two lighter cases raced up the stairs to get changed, hoping she had at least one presentable dress in one of the two cases, as she could hardly put in an appearance at the sort of restaurant Pierre would take her to in the casual slacks and tank top blouse that she wore.

She eventually located a dress that was not too creased in the earlier rush of packing, and was ready in well under the given time.

Her assumption of the type of restaurant Pierre would take her to proved correct, as within a short time they were drawing up outside the same plush establishment that he had taken her to the evening before, but what a lot had happened since then, she thought happily as her hand was caught in his as they walked towards the entrance.

'By the way,' Pierre said casually, 'what on earth gave you the idea that I was engaged to Paula?'

Cara's small hand tightened in his strong one. 'Something you said to me when you asked me to stay on at the villa,' she said as they went through to the dining room. She frowned in an effort of memory. 'You said you particularly wanted the place occupied at that time, or words to that effect, and I thought it was because of Paula.'

It was not a very lucid explanation, and she knew it, and waited for the inevitable comeback.

'I think, perhaps,' answered Pierre in an amused voice, 'that you'd better do a little more explaining, my love.'

Cara waited until the waiter had pulled out her chair and seated her before going on with the story. Oh, dear,' she sighed, 'I suppose I'd better confess all,' and went on to tell him about the London restaurant scene. 'I couldn't help overhearing what was said,' she explained. 'I was waiting for a friend of mine and she was late in turning up, and you were making a lot of noise at your table. Well,' she went on carefully, 'when someone teased you about your island bride, and how you ought to tell Paula about her,' she swallowed, 'I knew it was me they were talking about.'

Pierre nodded slowly. 'So that was it.' His eyes looked lovingly into hers. 'That explains why you tried so hard to keep your distance from me, and why you were so reluctant to take the villa. It must,' he said with a wicked grin, 'have been a shock when you discovered my identity.'

Cara smiled at this, then said gravely, 'Well, I can see the funny side of it now, but I was absolutely horrified at the time, I can assure you.' She gave him an accusing look. 'I do remember that you were amused, I probably had my mouth open.'

Pierre's grin widened showing his white even teeth. 'All I remember is that I thought you were adorable. I thought about you long after you were gone. I think,' he added on a more sober note, 'that that was why I was so furious with you when it looked as if you had some underhand scheme in mind. I felt let down—if that's the way to put it— I suppose I was half in love with you by then, and the thought of you being just another mercenary female was a bit hard to take, particularly as I had carefully made plans to ensure that I had a valid reason for keeping in touch with you by leasing you the villa.' His eyes twinkled again. 'I confess I did overdo the urgency of wanting the villa occupied. I had to put it that way so that you couldn't refuse me. And what did I get for my pains?' he added in mock dismay. 'Pushed into an engagement with another female!'

Cara's eyes travelled over his lean strong features. Just how well did he know Paula? she wondered.

Pierre saw the query in her eyes and caught her hand lying on the tablecloth. 'Not that well,' he said gently. 'Paula used me to keep her more persistent admirers at a distance. I was a great friend of her brother; we went to school together. Oh, I knew that she hoped that one day I would look on her as more than a friend, and because I escorted her to various social occasions many people thought that it was just a question of time. For my part,' he looked down at the gleaming silver on the table, 'well, I suppose my outlook on marital bliss was somewhat soured, in fact I didn't believe it existed outside of novels.'

He was silent for a few moments and Cara gave his hand a slight squeeze to show him that she understood his feelings. He looked up at her. 'I loved my mother, and I loved my father,' he said slowly, 'and it was inconceivable to me that they could ever part, they were so right for each other.' He gave a light shrug. 'But you know the story, it's as old as time. The affair didn't last either, that's what was so hurtful. A year perhaps, then it burnt itself out, but it was too late then, my mother was in France and there was no hope of a reconciliation, not on her part anyway. She had too much pride to take him back. Two wasted lives because a man could not resist a beautiful grasping siren.'

He turned Cara's hand over so that her palm was towards him and studied the delicate lines that criss-crossed over the palm. 'Falling in love with you has helped me to understand that part of it,' he said, his eyes leaving her palm and meeting hers. 'I want you in the same way I suppose my father must have wanted her. No matter if you were as she was, out to get every sou I possess.' He kissed her palm caressingly, making shivers of anticipation run down her spine. 'I have to thank providence that you are as sweet and as generous as the other one was mercenary and possessive. You proved that to me when you left the villa and tried to walk out of my life when you could have capitalised on the engagement announcement, only I wouldn't let you go—not now—not ever.'

Cara was grateful for the wine waiter's intervention just then as her heart was too full for words, but her thoughts were echoed in her lovely wide eyes as she sat back and listened to her one and only love order champagne.

Cara was never to remember just what the following meal consisted of, but she did remember standing under the stars a little while later with Pierre's arms around her and his demanding lips crushing hers, and in the midst of her new-found happiness came Maaua's teasing, but now prophetic remark, 'My granddaddy was never proved wrong!'